Troublemaker!

"Ma! Linda's cat is on the table, trying to get into the butter dish!" Joey yelled.

My mother came flying into the kitchen. "Get off of there!" she screamed. Scratchy jumped to the floor and tried to hide behind the legs of a chair.

"Get out of here! Get!" my mother yelled, grabbing a broom and chasing after Scratchy.

Poor Scratchy was terrified. She tried to get away by weaving through the maze of table and chair legs, but my mother kept swatting at her with the broom.

When Scratchy had run out of hiding places, she took a desperate leap from the floor to the washing machine.

Crash! My mother's favorite gardenia plant went flying to the floor. The pot shattered and dirt, leaves, and crushed gardenias scattered everywhere. . . .

Books by Linda Lewis

Want to Trade Two Brothers for a Cat?

Available from MINSTREL Books

2 Young 2 Go 4 Boys
We Hate Everything But Boys
Is There Life After Boys?
We Love Only Older Boys
My Heart Belongs to That Boy

Available from ARCHWAY Paperbacks

Want To Trade Two Brothers For A Cat?

Linda Lewis

A MINSTREL® BOOK

PUBLISHED BY POCKET BOOKS

New York   London   Toronto   Sydney   Tokyo

To Ira and Joey
the attorneys

A MINSTREL PAPERBACK *ORIGINAL*

 A Minstrel Book published by
POCKET BOOKS, a division of Simon & Schuster Inc.
1230 Avenue of the Americas, New York, NY 10020

ISBN: 0-671-66605-3

First Minstrel Books printing September 1989

10 9 8 7 6 5 4 3 2 1

Chapter One

It started on one of those rainy April days when my pesty brothers were really getting on my nerves. Ira and Joey are twins. They're just turning six, and they want everything I own. Take the brand-new comic books I had bought out of my own allowance. The brats can't even read yet, but they like to look at the pictures. I must have spent a good half-hour searching through our apartment before I found my comic books shoved under Joey's bed!

What really got me mad was that my brothers knew I was looking all over for those comics. You would think they would have had the decency to let me know where the comics were. But no, the two of them just sat there, right on Joey's bed, playing a game of Chutes and Ladders, as if my comics were nowhere near them.

"And just what are my comics doing under your bed, Joey Berman?" I demanded.

"Beats me." Joey's freckled face crinkled into a nasty grin.

"Maybe you put them there," Ira said, his brown eyes wide and innocent.

"Don't give me that garbage!" I said angrily. "I know you two were behind this. How many times do I have to tell you to keep away from my things?"

By that time I was tempted to go over and knock their twin heads together. But leave it to my brothers, they were saved by the bell. The phone rang, and my mother called out that it was for me.

"This better not happen again or else—or else you'll find you're missing pieces to every one of your stupid games!" I made sure to threaten them before I went to pick up the phone.

The call was not one that made me feel better. It was Brenda Roman—this girl who lives in my apartment building. Brenda was not my favorite person. I only played with her when I was absolutely desperate.

"I want you to come up to my house right away, Linda," Brenda demanded. "I'm *dying* to show you what my parents bought me. It's something special!"

"Oh, come on, Brenda. Your parents are always getting you something 'special.' To tell you the truth, I'm sick of looking at your new toys, new clothes, and new jewelry." Brenda was an only child, and if you asked me, she was spoiled rotten.

"This is not toys or clothes or jewelry. This really

is something special. I guarantee you'll love it, Linda!"

"Well, what is it?"

"I can't tell you. It would spoil the surprise. Just come on up and you'll see."

I stood there by the phone, trying to decide whether or not to go to Brenda's. I didn't want her to think I was overly anxious to see her latest possession. But part of me was curious to see what it was. And I certainly didn't want to hang around the house with my bratty brothers any longer.

I told my mother I was going to Brenda's. Then I took my time walking up the two flights of stairs to the fifth floor where Brenda lived.

Brenda's grandmother answered the door. She lives with Brenda and takes care of her while her parents work. I like Brenda's grandmother. She bakes the best apple cake I've ever tasted. "Go right into Brenda's room," she told me. "But go in very quietly. Pretty Boy startles easily."

Pretty Boy? Startles easily? I had no idea what Brenda's grandmother was talking about. Cautiously, I tapped on the door to Brenda's room.

"Is that you, Linda? Come on in."

I opened the door slowly and quietly, as instructed. There was brown-haired, beautiful Brenda, admiring her newest possession. Near her bed was a large cage on a stand. In it was a big parrot that began to talk as soon as it saw me: "Hello, hello. I'm Pretty Boy, Pretty Boy! *Awk! Awk! Awk!*"

3

"Mommy and Daddy brought him home for me last night," Brenda said proudly. "They wanted me to have company while they're away at work. Isn't he simply wonderful? The absolute best?"

Brenda thought everything she owned was the "absolute best." Ordinarily, I wouldn't have given her the satisfaction of letting her know how much I liked one of her things. But this time I couldn't help it. Pretty Boy was gorgeous. And when he talked, he sounded just like a person!

"Wow! He sure is great, Brenda!" I went over to look at Pretty Boy more closely. His feathers were bright green, red, and yellow. "Can you take him out of the cage?"

"Not yet. Daddy said I have to give him a few days to get used to it here before I let him out."

"Oh, that's too bad," I said. "I wonder if he'd learn to come to you and ride on your shoulder the way I saw a parrot do on TV."

"Of course he would. Pretty Boy is the smartest bird—aren't you, Pretty Boy?" As she said this, Brenda lifted the cage door just enough so she could slip in her hand. Pretty Boy hopped on it right away.

"Look at that! I bet that means he wants to get out," I said.

"I bet it does. And I'm sure a smart bird like Pretty Boy has had enough time to get used to it here already. I'm going to let him out!"

Brenda opened the cage door all the way and inched out her hand. Pretty Boy stayed perched on

4

it. He blinked his eyes and looked at Brenda and me.

"See, I knew he'd be just fine." Brenda proudly patted him on the head. "You want to pet him, Linda?"

"Sure." Cautiously, I reached out to touch his head. But as soon as my hand got close enough, Pretty Boy bent down and gave it a good, hard peck.

"Ow!" I pulled my hand back in pain.

"Awk! Awk! Awwwkk!" Pretty Boy let out three ear-piercing shrieks, then flapped his wings and took off flying around Brenda's room. He bumped into lamps and mirrors, and he knocked perfume bottles and hair clips off her dresser. Flying feathers filled the air.

"Look what you've done to my bird!" Brenda cried out.

"What I've done to *him!*" I sucked on the broken skin of my hand. "That bird is vicious!"

"He is not! And how am I ever going to get him back into his cage?" she wailed.

"By catching him and putting him back. But you'll have to do it by yourself. I've had enough of Pretty Boy for today and forever!" I started for the door of her room.

"No, Linda, you can't leave me now!" she cried. "You've got to help me get Pretty Boy back into his cage. He cost a fortune. My parents will kill me if they find out I let him out!" She gazed at me with pleading, frightened eyes.

"Oh, all right," I said reluctantly. "We have to

5

wait until he stops flying and settles somewhere. Then you come at him from one side, and I'll come from the other. When we get him cornered, you grab him and put him back in the cage."

Things started out just as I had planned them. Pretty Boy settled on Brenda's lamp and began grooming himself. Brenda and I crept slowly toward him. But just as Brenda was about to grab him, her grandmother opened the door, carrying a tray with apple cake and two big glasses of milk on it.

"How would you girls like some ca—*aake!*" Her question turned into a shriek as Pretty Boy took off for the open doorway. His wings brushed her head as he flew out the door.

Brenda's grandmother lost her grip on the tray, and it went crashing to the floor. Glass shattered, milk spilled, and cake crumbled all over.

For a moment, the three of us stood staring at the mess on the floor. Then we forgot about the mess as Brenda began to scream in horror.

"Oh no! Oh no! The living-room window is partway open! If Pretty Boy flies out we'll never get him back!"

It wasn't easy to recapture Pretty Boy, and, if you asked me, it wasn't even desirable. I couldn't see why Brenda would want that bird now that we knew how vicious he was. It was only because of Brenda's grandmother, who felt awful for having let Pretty Boy out of the room, that I decided to help.

The first thing I did was run to shut the living-room window before Pretty Boy could fly out. Then, because Brenda was too busy carrying on to be useful, I came up with the next plan of action.

"Stand in the doorway to the living room to keep Pretty Boy inside," I told Brenda and her grandmother. "I'll go get something to help capture him."

I raced back to Brenda's room and looked around for—well, I didn't really know what would be good for catching birds. Something I could throw over Pretty Boy. Something I could wrap around him so he wouldn't peck me to shreds while I was carrying him back to his cage.

I knew—a sheet! I went to Brenda's perfectly made bed and unmade it. I pulled the sheet right off her mattress and ran with it into the living room.

"What are you doing with my designer sheet?" Brenda asked.

"I need it to catch your designer bird," I answered. "But if the sheet's more important, I'll put it back."

"No, no. Just get my Pretty Boy! He's what I really care about." Brenda sighed.

By this time, Pretty Boy had perched upon the head of a marble statue in one corner of the room. He was trying to pull a loose feather from his tail and seemed to be ignoring us. It was the perfect time to get him.

Brenda's grandmother kept guard at the door-

7

way. Brenda and I followed our original plan of coming at Pretty Boy from two different sides. When we got close enough I took aim and tossed the sheet over Pretty Boy.

What a fight that bird put up! Squawking and pecking and squirming to get out of that sheet. Wrapping the sheet around him, I ran with him to Brenda's room and tossed him, sheet and all, into the cage.

It didn't take long for Pretty Boy to fight his way out of the sheet. Except for a few ruffled feathers, he was none the worse for his experience.

Brenda's sheet, however, was another story. Pretty Boy had paid it the ultimate insult, as Brenda found out when she went to remove it by reaching her hand into the cage.

"Ugh! There's bird-do all over!" She dropped the offending sheet to the floor.

She rushed to the bathroom to wash her hands. "This is all your fault, Linda," she said when she returned. "If you hadn't made me take Pretty Boy out of his cage, this never would have happened. And I know it's all because you're jealous of me, too. I want you to get out of here now, and never come play with me again!"

"No problem. I was just about to leave, anyway," I said. Then I glanced at Brenda and began to laugh aloud.

"What's so funny?" she asked angrily.

"Your sh-shoulder." I struggled to get the words

out between peals of laughter. "Pretty Boy seems to have left you a present on your sh-shoulder!"

Brenda looked where I was pointing and let out a scream. "Grandma! Come help me! Pretty Boy got bird-do all over my brand-new designer shirt!"

Chapter Two

I laughed all the way home from Brenda's house. The expression on her face when she looked at her shoulder was one of the funniest things I'd ever seen! And it served her right, too. The nerve of her, blaming me for what happened with Pretty Boy. She was the one who took him out of the cage so she could show off!

But late that night, thinking about what had happened, I no longer found it so funny. I was lying in bed, in my room that I shared with my brothers, when I found this strange sadness coming over me.

It wasn't because Brenda was mad at me. I didn't care if she never wanted to be my friend again. After all, I was a tomboy. I kept my light brown hair cut short and wore jeans and T-shirts whenever possible. The friends I really cared about were all boys—Danny, Teddy, and Billy. I would rather run and climb and play ball with them than be around stuck-up Brenda any day.

No, I was sad because, for the first time, Brenda really did have something I wanted. Something I had always wanted—a pet of my own.

But I didn't want my pet to be a vicious bird like Brenda's, either. Oh, no. The pet I wanted was a dog. A dog who would always be there for me, no matter what. If I had a dog, I would never be lonely.

My tenth birthday was coming in June. What would be a better gift than a dog for my birthday? I decided to approach my parents the very next day to drop some gentle hints. They would probably need some time to get used to the idea.

I tried Mom first. I waited until I figured she'd be in a good mood—when she was in the kitchen preparing dinner. Mom loves to cook. She's got some very old-fashioned ideas about things, including food. She won't use anything canned or frozen, if she can help it. Fresh is best, even if it's twice the work.

I started with the indirect approach. "Can you believe I'm going to be ten soon, Ma? That's double digits! I know they don't call it that, but do you realize ten is technically zero-teen?"

"Uh-huh." Mom nodded pleasantly, her dark eyes focused on the pile of green beans on the table before her.

"I was thinking, Ma," I went on. "Now that I'm almost a teenager, it's time I learned to be more responsible. And do you know what would teach me to be the most responsible of all? Taking care of

11

a pet, like a dog, for example. A dog would be the perfect gift for my birthday. What do you say, Ma?"

Mom's hands froze in the act of cutting the beans into bite-size pieces. "Linda Berman, I don't know where you came up with a ridiculous idea like getting a dog. A small, two-bedroom, New York City apartment is no place for an animal. There's hardly enough room here for our family as it is!"

"There would be—if we didn't have Ira and Joey!" I said hotly.

"Come on, Linda. Stop that nonsense!" There was a warning note in my mother's voice. She hated it when I said anything bad about her precious twins.

But I knew I was right. I remember clearly what life was like before Ira and Joey were born. I was the only child. Everyone thought I was the greatest kid ever. Then my brothers came along and spoiled everything!

Being twins made Ira and Joey special. They didn't look alike—Ira was taller and had straight hair; Joey had curly hair and freckles. Still, my mother dressed them alike. She pushed them around when they were little in this big double stroller. Everyone stopped to fuss over them.

"Oooh, look—twins! Aren't they adorable? Oooh, they smiled; ooh, they said 'ga-ga'; ooh, they walked! Oooh! Oooh! Oooh!"

It made me sick. Actually, about the only thing that Ira and Joey did that other babies didn't do was develop this trick of one finishing a sentence

12

the other started. No big deal. Still, the fact that they were twins made everyone pay them extra attention, and me that much less.

Besides all that, Ira and Joey really were the reason we were stuck in this small apartment. We could afford to move to a three-bedroom apartment where I could have a room of my own if Mom would go to work. But she believes it's important for a mother to be at home during her children's "formative" years. She says she'll consider working once my brothers start first grade, but only at a part-time job so she can be home when we come back from school.

At that rate, I can see us stuck in this apartment forever. I'll always have to share a room with my brothers, and I'll never be able to get my dog. And all because of pesty Ira and Joey. Boy, I'd give anything to be able to trade my brothers in for a pet. Too bad there weren't places you could go and do it!

I gave up on Mom and decided to devote my energies to Dad. I waited until after dinner so he would have a chance to unwind after work. He was sitting in the living room, watching the news. Mom was cleaning up in the kitchen, and my brothers were in our room, so I would have Dad all to myself. As soon as the commercial went on, I sprung into action.

"Dad." I sat next to him on the sofa and kind of snuggled up to him. "You know what I'm missing most in my life? A companion."

"A companion?"

"Uh-huh. You know. Someone to be there when I need a friend—always ready to play when I am."

"But Linda, you have plenty of friends. There's Danny and Teddy and Billy. Even though they're all boys." Dad smiled at me and his blue-gray eyes that were much like my own, twinkled. Fortunately, he accepts the fact I'm a tomboy.

"Friends are not what I'm talking about. I mean a *real* companion. Someone to be with me all the time and keep me from being lonely. Someone to hold on to and cuddle and really love. I need a dog!"

"A dog!" Dad's bushy eyebrows drew together in a frown. I ignored that and smiled my most charming smile.

"That's right, Daddy. I knew you'd understand. All kids should have dogs to keep them company, especially when they're turning ten and becoming responsible. I'll take care of my dog really well, Daddy—honest!" I gazed at him with pleading eyes.

Dad usually softens when I call him *Daddy;* this time was no exception. He stopped frowning and got this regretful look on his face. "Taking care of a dog is only part of the problem, Linda. The fact is that being cooped up in a city apartment is not a good life for a dog. It wouldn't be fair to the animal."

I was about to try another approach when my mother came in from the kitchen. "Animal? Are you still carrying on about wanting a dog, Linda? I

14

told you this afternoon that there isn't room in the apartment. It's absolutely out of the question!"

I looked from Mom to Dad. There they were—a united front. Maybe separately I could have convinced them, but together I didn't stand a chance.

I had lost this round; I could see that. But I wasn't ready to give up yet. I wanted a dog so badly. There had to be a way!

Chapter
Three

By mid-April, it became obvious to me that my parents were not going to give in on the issue of the dog. As unhappy as I was about this, at least there was something to make me feel better. It was spring, and that meant life was beginning to pick up again.

In the warm weather, I hardly even saw Brenda. I was often out playing ball with Danny, Teddy, and Billy, and sometimes other kids from our block. We rigged up all sorts of games in the street. We played basketball through the rungs of a fire-escape ladder. We played "stoopball" in the courtyard of my building: You run around the bases and score the game just like baseball—the difference is you throw the ball against the corner of the stoop instead of hitting it with a bat. You don't need a pitcher or a catcher that way, which is good because there are never enough kids for two full teams.

With all that was going on, I eased up nagging

about the dog. I still dropped hints now and then, like whenever I saw a kid walking a dog. But my parents would give me their "We told you there's no room for a dog in our apartment" routine every time. It seemed as if I were getting nowhere.

Then, just as I thought all was lost, Dad came up with this wonderful idea. A dog was not a good pet for an apartment, but there was a chance a cat might work out. Teddy's little brother, Fred, had found a cat named Tabby that was about to give birth to kittens. If I would be happy with a kitten, Fred's mother was willing to let me have first pick of the litter.

Would I be happy with a kitten? Suddenly, all thoughts about dogs were removed from my mind. Kittens were cute and cuddly and lovable. You didn't have to take them out for walks on snowy and rainy days. I don't know why I hadn't thought of a kitten myself. A kitten was a perfect pet for an apartment!

"I'd love a kitten, Daddy!" I said happily.

"Okay. Then I'll tell your mother to make the arrangements. But you have to understand one thing, Linda. We're taking this kitten on a trial basis at first. If, for any reason, it isn't working out to have a kitten in our home, we'll have to give it away. Can you accept that condition?"

"Sure, Daddy," I said easily. I couldn't see any reason why a kitten wouldn't work out. I was so thrilled and excited by the idea of having my own kitten. It was almost too good to be true!

The very first person I told my good news to was Danny Kopler. Danny lived in the apartment above mine, so we were together a lot. I really like Danny, but he has some strange ways about him. For one thing, he's a genius. He's just eleven years old, but he's in sixth grade, and he's already doing calculus. He taught it to himself. Thinks it's great fun. Every time I go up to his house, there's Danny standing in front of his big green blackboard, working out some sort of equation.

Now that stuff has its place, but it's getting so that Danny would rather do math than play ball. It shows on him, too. He's starting to get pretty fat around his middle. Anyhow, on the day I went to tell Danny my news, I found him at the blackboard as usual, drawing lines and X's and Y's all over the place.

At first he didn't seem too glad to see me. I guess I interrupted his concentration or something. But when I told him about the kitten, he looked interested.

"A kitten?" he said. "What do you know about taking care of a kitten?"

"What's there to know? You feed it cat food and give it a litter box so it can go to the bathroom. At least that's what Teddy says Fred does with Tabby."

"Teddy says Fred does—humph!" Danny snorted. "Do you want a dumb ordinary cat like Tabby? Or do you want this one to be something special?"

18

"It is going to be something special," I insisted. "Because it's going to be *my* kitten."

"I mean besides that." He looked disgusted, as if I were some sort of dumb girl. Usually I can't stand it when Danny gets in these ridiculous superior moods. But today I was too excited to even pay attention.

"Don't you see this is the perfect opportunity to try a scientifically controlled experiment?" Excitedly, he ran his fingers through his dirty-blond hair, making it stick up in little tufts all over. "We can raise a super cat!"

"A super cat?"

"Yup. We can start from the day it's born. Give it proper training. Teach it tricks. How to respond to commands. Like scientists do with rats in a maze."

"Rats in a maze? Just what do you mean by that, Danny?" I wasn't sure I liked the sound of this at all.

"You know. Do experiments. You get the cat real hungry and only give it food when it performs the way you want it to. It's called positive reinforcement—you reward it when it does little things you want. You put the little things together to make a big thing. If you can teach a rat, there's no reason why you can't teach a kitten."

"Oh, yes, there is a reason," I insisted.

"Oh, yeah? What?"

"Me."

"You?"

"Yes, me. I'm not going to let you torture my kitten by depriving him of food. Or any other scheme you might dream up for that matter," I said firmly.

Danny looked at me, surprised I would dare go against him. Usually, I'm so glad to be around him that I go along with whatever he wants to do. But this time was different. This was my kitten we were talking about!

"But, it's for the sake of science," Danny said.

"I don't care about science! I'm not going to let you turn my kitten into a laboratory rat!"

He looked thoughtful. "Well, maybe laboratory rat wasn't the right way to put it," he admitted. "But I still think that if you're going to raise a kitten, you ought to try to make him the best kitten you can. Am I wrong?"

"No. I can go along with that—so far."

"Good. So since we agree on that, we can set about discovering the most effective ways to make sure he's best."

"How do we do that?" I was still suspicious of Danny's motives.

"I'll tell you what. Tomorrow's Saturday. We'll go to the library and take out every book on cats, kittens, and raising animals. Then we can make an educated decision."

That sounded reasonable to me. So I agreed to go to the library with Danny. In fact, I was looking forward to it. It was a way to bring me closer to having my very own kitten!

Chapter
Four

On Saturday morning, as I got ready to go to the library, all these wonderful thoughts ran through my head: I would get the cat books and find out all about kittens; I would draw some cat pictures and put them up over my bed. These kind of things would make the time go faster until I could bring my kitten home to live with me.

"Ma, I'm going to the library to do some research on cats," I called as I walked by the kitchen. Mom was busy with one of her domestic projects. She was baking her own bread, made from whole-wheat flour and nuts and seeds. Very healthy.

"Sounds like a good idea, Linda." She pushed her black hair back from her face. "Just be back in time for lunch."

"Sure. See you later." I grabbed my stack of library books that were due back soon anyway and headed for the door. The big thing now was to escape before my brothers realized where I was going.

No such luck. Those little brats were in our room, but they heard me from clear across the apartment. They dashed into the kitchen and started making their demands. "Ma, we want to go to the library, too. Make Linda take us with her, Ma!"

"Oh, no," I said immediately. "You're not coming with me—not this time." The last time I took my brothers to the library they spent a whole hour choosing their books. I had to wait for them the entire time. "Go to the library by yourselves!"

"Linda, you know there are two very bad crossings on the way to the library." Mom made sure to remind me of this. "I didn't even let you go by yourself until you were nine. So it's not so terrible if you take your brothers with you."

"But it is, Ma," I pleaded with her. "Danny's going with me to help me do cat research. We don't want little pests getting in our way."

"Did you hear that, Ma?" said Ira.

"Linda called us pests—for no good reason," said Joey.

Mom shook her head and went back to kneading her bread. "Your brothers are right, Linda. There's no reason to start name-calling. Now just take them with you, or Danny can go to the library by himself."

So Ira and Joey got their way again. Of course, Mom didn't see it when the brats stuck their tongues out at me as soon as her back was turned. My brothers get away with everything!

When we got to the library, I deposited Ira and Joey in the picture-book section. Danny and I went to look up cat books.

We found a stack of books, brought them to a table and began to look them over. Danny began taking notes as fast as he could and calling out all these facts and statistics.

"Wow! Look at this! Cats see better at night because their eyes are covered with something called guanine. It also makes their eyes glow at night. And their ears have almost thirty muscles, compared to six in man. They can turn their ears in the direction of a sound, even faster than a dog can.

"Hey! If you cut off a cat's whiskers, it's temporarily incapacitated. Hmm——I wonder just exactly what that means. What if we——"

"Danny!" I knew exactly what he had in mind. "We're not going to cut off my cat's whiskers!"

"But——it's for science!"

"Forget it!"

"Well, okay. But here are some statistics you should be interested in. The gestation period for cats averages sixty-three to sixty-five days."

"What's a gestation period?" I asked.

"How long the mother cat is pregnant before the babies are born. Fred's had Tabby for over a month now, and the cat was pregnant when he found her.

23

So that means it's got to be within the next few weeks that your kitten will be born. It could be any day, even!"

"Any day—wow! I can't believe it. I could have my kitten so soon!"

"You can't. Even if it's born now, the book says you can't take it away from its mother for at least two months. The mother has to feed it and teach it stuff."

"Then it looks like I'll be getting the kitten around my birthday after all—that's on June 20th. And even if I have to wait, it doesn't matter. I can pick out the one I want right from the time it's born. I can visit it and let it get used to me right away."

"Not if you want to be sure to get the cutest one," Danny informed me. "It says right here that kittens may not develop their permanent markings for weeks. The cutest might turn out to be the ugliest and vice versa."

"Then how do I know which one to pick?" All these statistics were confusing.

Danny shrugged. "Well, if you can hold off making a decision for a month or so, you'll know what the kittens will look like. If you can't—well, maybe you'll get lucky and pick the best one. And if it turns out you don't like it very much—we can still use it for scientific purposes."

"Danny! You're not using my cat for scientific anything!" I reminded him. I guess I must have spoken too loudly, because people working at neighboring tables began staring at us and giving us dirty looks.

"Let's go, Danny." I began gathering up the cat books. "We can check these out and look at them at home."

"Okay. But before we leave, I want to pick up a couple of books on calculus."

So I had to wait for Danny to get his books. Then I had to wait for Ira and Joey, because this time they had each picked seven books, and you were only allowed to check out six. They couldn't make up their minds which ones to put back.

It seemed like forever before I got my cat books to the check-out counter.

"Only two," the librarian announced to me. "You can only take out two of these books."

"But why?" I asked. "My brothers got to take out six."

"Yes, but those were fiction books." The librarian explained: "If it's factual books, you're only allowed two on a particular subject. It keeps our shelves from being depleted."

"But—I need them," I protested. "I'm getting a cat of my own soon. A brand-new baby kitten."

"I'm glad to hear that." The librarian adjusted the glasses on her nose. "But you'll just have to read the rest of the books here. Two are all you're allowed to take home, and that's that."

So now I had to stand there deciding which two books I wanted most.

"Hurry up," Ira urged me impatiently.

"Yeah, we're sick of having to wait for you all the time," added Joey.

Wait for *me* all the time—what nerve! I was strongly tempted to tell my brothers exactly what I thought of them right there and then. But there was already a line of people forming behind me, waiting to check out books. So I controlled myself and chose the two books with the most pictures, instead of giving my brothers what they deserved.

After all, my kitten was going to be born soon, and that was what really mattered.

Chapter Five

One week later, Teddy came to my door with the news: "They're here, Linda! They're here! Three of them. Born ten o'clock this morning. They don't even look like kittens!"

"Of course not. Kittens are born blind, deaf, and helpless." I told Teddy some of the information I had picked up during my three trips back to the library. I bet I knew more about cats than almost anybody.

Teddy stared at me. "Well, don't you want to see them?"

"See them?" For a moment it didn't register with me that the day I had been waiting for had finally come. I could actually go and see my kitten. Right now, right this minute! "Can I really? Are you sure your mom won't mind?"

"No." Teddy laughed. "She told me you could come over and take a look."

"Great! Hang on, Teddy. I just have to tell my

mother!" I went bursting into my mother's bed-room, where I found her stooped over the sewing machine. She was making some summer shorts for my brothers and me.

"Ma! The kittens are born! The kittens are born!" I announced joyfully. "And Teddy's mother says I can go see them! Okay, Ma?"

My mother looked up from her sewing. "Okay. But don't stay too long. I'm sure the mother cat doesn't want to be bothered so soon after giving birth."

"I won't," I said, already heading toward the front door. As I passed my room, the dreaded thing happened: Ira and Joey came rushing out and started making their demands.

"Ma! We heard Linda say the kittens were born. We want to see them, too. Make her take us with her, Ma. Make her!"

I knew it was coming, but this time I played it smart. I picked up speed and reached the front door just as I heard my mother's voice: "Linda, why don't you take your brothers with you?"

"Come on, Teddy—quick!" I said to him as I raced off toward the hallway staircase. This was one great moment I refused to let the terrible twins spoil for me!

Even after all my reading, I wasn't prepared for the sight of those tiny little creatures. If I hadn't known they were kittens, I never would have believed it. They looked more like blind mice than cats.

But Tabby cat knew they were hers. She kept them cuddled up next to her, and she licked them all over. That was to clean them and help stimulate their circulation. I remembered reading about that.

"Aren't they something?" seven-year-old Fred said proudly. "I wish I could keep them all, but Mom says no way. She's already promised one to you and the others to my cousins in New Jersey. So at least I'll get to see them sometimes when I go visiting."

"And you can see mine whenever you like, Fred," I said.

"Good!" said Fred. "Then I'm glad you're getting first pick. My cousin, Raymond, was mad when he heard Mom had told you that. But she said that a promise is a promise and that Raymond would have to pick second."

"Oh," I said uncomfortably. "I don't want to cause trouble with your family."

"Don't you worry about that, Linda." Mrs. Pappas, Teddy and Fred's mother, came into the room. "Cousin Raymond has got a lot to learn about things like patience and respecting the rights of others. He'll just have to accept picking second for a change. You get first choice." She smiled at me, and I felt better. Mrs. Pappas is tops as far as mothers go. She always seems to know what to say to make kids feel okay.

"I don't think I'm ready to choose yet, though," I said to her.

"That's not surprising." She laughed. "These kittens have a lot of growing to do before you can even tell what they're going to look like. I'll tell you what. You can come visit the kittens whenever you like so you get to know them. You don't have to make your choice until you're ready to take your kitten home."

"Really? That's terrific!" I couldn't believe my good luck. By the time the kittens were ready to leave their mother, I would know which one was the best.

It took weeks before the kittens started looking like real kittens. Then their eyes opened, and they could see. They moved around and climbed over their mother and each other. They made little squealing noises. And they began to get patterns in their fur.

By the time they were a month old, they were developing their own looks and personalities. One was smoke-gray, with gray eyes, the runt of the litter. It always stayed close to its mother. Another was gray tiger-striped with green eyes. It was always hungry, always trying to get more food from its mother, even if it had to shove the other kittens out of the way. And the third was white with dark splotches on its back and head and had deep blue eyes. It was the curious playful one, always trying to poke its way out of the box and into the world. And clumsy! Half the time it tried to do something it would wind up falling and bumping its nose.

I grew to love all of them in different ways. The little smokey-gray one made me feel soft and tender. The tiger was fun because he was so tough and adventurous. And the splotchy one was so funny it always made me laugh.

How was I ever going to choose between them when the time came?

One day, when I was at Teddy's, playing with the kittens, his cousin, Raymond, came over. Raymond was ten, like Teddy, but he was bigger and fatter. He had a red face and little squinty eyes. He frowned and his eyebrows almost met in the middle of his forehead. I disliked him right away.

"So you're the one who's getting first pick of the kittens," he said nastily.

"That's right," I replied. "The pick of the litter."

"Well this lousy litter isn't much to pick from," he said with a snort. "That gray is just a puny runt. It'll probably die, anyhow. The tiger at least looks strong, but it's nothing but a common alley cat. And this one"—"he pointed to the splotched kitten who had finally just about made it up to the top of the box—"this one is too darn wild." He laughed his evil laugh and gave the kitten such a hard slap that it went flying over the top of the box. It stood where it landed, looking around wildly and mewing away.

I rushed over to the poor frightened kitten and picked it up. It was so scared it gave a yowl and dug its claws into me, making little scratches on the back of my hand. But I held on to it anyway, patting it and talking to it soothingly. "Don't dig your claws in me, you little scratchy thing. Be a nice kitten, a good kitten." I felt it starting to relax in my arms. It snuggled against me and soon was mewing happily. That's when I knew this kitten was the one I wanted.

I looked up to where Raymond stood watching me, grinning his evil grin. "Don't you ever put your grubby hands on this kitten again!" I exclaimed. "His name is Scratchy and he's mine!"

Chapter Six

My tenth birthday was the very best birthday of my life. It wasn't because of the party my parents made me, although that was nice, too—Danny, Billy, Teddy, and even little Fred were invited, and Brenda Roman wasn't. It wasn't because of the cake Mom baked or the presents I got, or because for one day I was treated as more special than my brothers. This birthday was the best because the moment I had been waiting for was finally arriving. The day after my party was the day I got to take Scratchy home with me.

Danny came along with me to help figure out the most scientific way of transporting the kitten from Teddy's house to mine. I let Ira and Joey come along with me because I was in such a great mood about taking my kitten home that I didn't even mind having them around.

I was a little disappointed in what Danny came up with for a cat-carrier. It was this cardboard carton he'd had in his closet, which he'd poked some holes in for air. He had threaded a piece of rope through the carton so that the ends formed two handles for carrying. That was it. I had been hoping for something a little classier for Scratchy, but I didn't say anything. I didn't want to hurt Danny's feelings, and it wasn't such a long walk from Teddy's building to mine, anyhow.

When we arrived at Teddy's, Raymond was there. He had come to take his kitten home, too. The one he didn't pick would go to another cousin from New Jersey. I sure hoped that that cousin was nicer than Raymond.

Raymond gave me a dirty look when he saw me. Then he looked at Mrs. Pappas and began to whine. "It's not fair that you're giving her first choice of the kittens. I'm family and she's not!"

"Now, Raymond, cut that out," Mrs. Pappas said in a sweet voice. I couldn't help wondering how she could sound so nice when talking to Raymond. If I were his aunt I would slap him in the face. In fact, if I were just a little bigger, I would slap him in the face! "I promised Linda first pick, and that's that," she said. "Which kitten did you decide on, Linda?"

I looked at the little smokey-gray, still so weak and helpless, and my heart went out to it. What if Raymond picked it? It wouldn't last long with a rotten creep like Raymond. The tiger, at least, was strong and could fend for itself. It was stalking a little fuzz ball across the floor right now, and it was really adorable, too. I loved both of those kittens.

But when I looked at Scratchy racing around the room in his crazy, funny way, I knew that there was only one choice for me. I picked Scratchy up, and he rubbed his soft head against me and began purring away.

"This one," I said firmly. "And I've decided to name him Scratchy."

"You've decided to name *her* Scratchy." Teddy's mother smiled. "This kitten is a girl."

"She is?" I looked at tough little Scratchy, and it was hard to believe it. "Then she must be a tomboy, just like me!"

"Well, whatever she is, she's a wild thing," said Raymond. "You'll see. You'll be sorry you picked her when she gets away from you and is run over by a car—splat! Flat cat!" He laughed viciously.

"Raymond! What a terrible thing to say!" Teddy's mother looked at Raymond angrily.

Raymond didn't seem to care whom he made angry. He went over and picked up the tiger-striped kitten. "Tiger is the one for me. He's no sissy girl cat, right, Tiger?" He held Tiger up under his front legs and shook him in the air. Tiger squirmed so hard to get away he shot out from Raymond's hands and scooted under Teddy's bed.

We all laughed as Raymond squatted down and tried to get Tiger out from under the bed. But Raymond was too fat to fit under there with Tiger. And every time Raymond ran to one side of the bed, Tiger would race over to the other. That made me glad about one thing at least! If any kitten could stand up to Raymond, it was Tiger.

It was a big struggle just to get Scratchy into the carrying case Danny had made. She squirmed and fought so hard that my hands had brand-new scratches on them by the time we got her into the box. Danny taped the lid shut. He held on to the rope carrying-handle on one end, and I took the other. I said thank you to Teddy's mother and to Fred, and we set off toward my house, walking very slowly.

For once I was glad I had Ira and Joey with me. They opened the doors for us and watched where we were going on the sidewalk so we didn't bump into things. Danny and I were kept busy trying to balance the box and make sure Scratchy didn't get out.

Inside the box, Scratchy was making plenty of noise. It sounded like she was running from one end to another, searching for a way out. She kept mewing and pushing up against the flap of the box. I was scared to death she'd escape, right there in the street, and get run over by a car the way Raymond had predicted.

Billy Upton, who lives in the building across the street, spotted us as we entered my courtyard. "What in the world do you have there?" he asked. Billy's two years older than I am, and he can be a bully. Sometimes he acts almost like Raymond.

That's when I don't like him much. Other times he can be really nice though, so I try to overlook the off days. But I wasn't so sure I wanted Billy around Scratchy.

I was trying to think of something to tell him so he would go away when my blabbermouth brothers piped up. "It's a kitten. One of Fred's cat's litter. We're taking it home for the first time."

"A kitten! Let's see!" Billy grabbed for the carrying case.

"Don't—" I began, but Billy paid me no attention. Billy was big, Billy was strong, and Billy was fast. Before I could do anything to stop him, he had untaped the lid of the carrying case and stuck his hand inside.

I don't know what Billy was expecting to happen when he did this, but he deserved what happened next. Scratchy must have figured this strange hand was somehow attacking her. She did the logical thing under the circumstances—she attacked it back.

"Ye-ow!" Billy let out a yell of pain. He pulled his hand out of the carton and began waving it in the air. "It scratched me!"

I wanted to tell him that Scratchy would never have scratched him if he hadn't been so dumb and stuck his hand in the carton, but I didn't have the time. Now that Billy had opened the tape, I knew it wouldn't take much for Scratchy to fight her way out of the carton. Holding down the lid as best I could, I took off running toward the entrance to my building. Danny hung on to his end of the rope and struggled to keep up with me.

"Get the doors—quick!" I shouted to my brothers. For once, they listened. Ira opened the door to the building, and Joey raced ahead and opened the door to my apartment, as Danny, Billy, and I stumbled up the stairs.

It was perfect timing. Scratchy squirmed her way out of the carton just as we burst into my apartment. Fortunately, she ran forward instead of backward, so we all managed to file inside and close the door safely behind us.

"She's heading for our room!" Ira pointed excitedly.

"Get her!" I gasped. "Before she goes under a bed!"

But it was too late. Even as I spoke, Scratchy dashed directly under Ira's bed.

"I'll get her out of there!" Joey shouted.

"No, I will!" Billy shoved him aside.

"Hey, not so fast—remember to set about things scientifically!" Danny protested.

After that, I couldn't hear what anyone was saying because everyone was talking at once. Everyone was pushing to get under Ira's bed and be the one to get Scratchy out.

"Hey! What's going on in here? Why are you making so much noise?" It was my mother's voice that was heard above the racket.

"It's Scratchy, Ma," I explained. "No sooner did she get out of her carrying case than she escaped and ran under Ira's bed. We're trying to figure out the best way to get her out."

Mom shook her head. "Well, I can tell you one thing for sure. What you're doing now is positively the worst way. That poor kitten is scared stiff. Leaving her mother, being thrust into a new environment. And then all you strange giants—you are giants to a little kitten, you know—running about and making so much noise. Wouldn't you want to be under the bed if you were a kitten?"

"Oh." I realized Mom was right. I don't know why I hadn't been able to see for myself that Scratchy was scared, and we were making things worse for her. "Well, what should we do then to get her out?"

"Nothing right now," said Mom. "Let her be, so she realizes she's safe. Later on, we'll put some food and water where she can get to it—and her litter box. But for now, let's just leave her alone. Danny, Billy, I think it's best for you boys to go home now. You can come back tomorrow when Scratchy has a chance to get used to it here."

"Okay, Mrs. Berman," Danny and Billy said at the same time.

"You can keep the cat-carrier I made, Linda," Danny said on his way out. "You never know when it might come in handy."

"I'm not going to use that thing anymore," I said.

"I'm going to teach Scratchy to come outside with me and not run away."

Danny glanced over to Ira's bed, where the tip of Scratchy's tail could be seen poking out from underneath the covers. "Fat chance," he said.

But that only made me even more determined.

Chapter
Seven

I can't say that Scratchy's first night in our apartment went well. Poor Scratchy must have missed her mother because she cried and howled the whole night.

Even though it was his bed Scratchy was under, Ira slept like a baby. Joey did, too. It was I who was up all night, checking to make sure Scratchy was all right.

I know that if she had slept with me in my bed, things would have been different. I would have cuddled her just like her mother would have done. I would have made her understand that everything was all right. But Scratchy wouldn't let me near her. Every time I peeked under Ira's bed, Scratchy went scooting off to the far corner so I couldn't reach her. So I just went back to bed again and tried to sleep.

By morning, I was exhausted. It was a good thing it was Saturday, so I didn't have to get up for school.

I was lying there, half-asleep, when Mom poked her head into my room.

"I don't know how you slept the whole night, Linda. I could hear that kitten crying all the way from my bedroom."

"Oh, I managed," I said. I forced myself to sit up in bed and look lively.

"I slept fine." Ira sat up in his bed and yawned.

"Let's see how Scratchy is doing." Joey jumped out of his bed and bent down to look under Ira's. "She's still there."

"Of course she's still there," I grumbled, kneeling down next to him. There was Scratchy, still huddled in the corner where I had last seen her. "That's the problem. She's not coming out to go anyplace else. She didn't even touch her food or water."

"Or her litter box," Mom said. "And that's why you're going to have to get her out from under the bed right away, Linda. If she should have an accident on the rug, it's almost impossible to get out the odor."

"Don't worry, Mom. I'll get her out." My mind was racing, trying to think up the best way to go about this.

Ira's bed was in one corner of our room. He always liked the security of sleeping close to the wall. That made Scratchy a lot harder to get to, so I figured the best thing to do would be to move the bed away from the wall. Chances were that she would start to run when I did that, and that's where having two brothers might come in handy.

"Ira," I said, "you take a post along one wall. Joey, you stand along the other. When I pull out this bed, she's got to run toward one of you."

For a change, my brothers cooperated with me, each taking a spot by the wall. I took a deep breath, then quickly pulled the bed toward the center of the room. I waited to see in which direction Scratchy would run.

To my surprise, she chose neither. She was so frightened she didn't move at all. She just pressed her body way back into the corner and huddled there, staring at me through wide blue eyes.

I was tempted to rush right over and grab her, but something made me take it slow. "Everyone stay right where you are," I warned them. I eased myself down on the bed and inched my hand over toward Scratchy's body. She tried to press still farther into the corner, but other than that she didn't move. She was letting me stroke her fur!

After a while, she seemed to relax. She even began to purr. "She's purring, Ma," I said. "She's letting me pet her."

Mom sighed. "That's wonderful, Linda, but it still doesn't solve the basic problem. That cat is going to have to use the litter box soon and if—"

"How're things going in here?" Dad's question interrupted her.

"Fine, Daddy," I said quickly. "Scratchy's letting me pet her."

"Not so fine at all," said Mom. "The cat's been crying all night long—I'm surprised you were able to sleep. But what's worse is that she still hasn't come out from under the bed. Which means she has not yet used the litter box."

"Did you try offering her some food?" asked Dad.

"We left some dry food right by the bed." Ira pointed to the small dish of cat food.

"Dry food!" Dad exclaimed. "No wonder the cat's not coming out. Would you bother leaving your bed for some dry cat food? I bet something more enticing would do the trick. Why don't you run down to the grocery store, Linda, and get some of that nice canned cat food?"

"Great idea, Dad!" I don't think I ever got dressed so fast or went to the store so willingly in my life. I came back with a can of special tuna-fish cat food.

Dad's idea was a good one. Scratchy sniffed the tuna that Dad held out to her and began slowly creeping toward him. As she got closer to the can, Dad moved it back a little so she had to come a little farther. When she was totally out in the open, Dad put some tuna fish down in her bowl on top of the dry cat food.

Scratchy took a look around, and I guess she figured we were not that dangerous after all. Either that or she was really hungry. In any case, she began to eat up the tuna. Once she had eaten that, she finished off the dry cat food as well. We all stood back and watched, careful not to scare her away.

"Give her something to drink now," whispered Joey.

"She's got water right there if she wants it," I said.

"Water! She probably doesn't care for water, either," said Dad, who seemed all proud of himself now that his canned-cat-food scheme had worked. "That kitten probably wants something better— like milk."

"'Cow's milk is not an appropriate drink for kittens.'" I quoted what I had read in one of my cat books. "'It sometimes causes gastric disturbances that are difficult to remedy.'"

"Oh, listen to her." Both twins groaned in unison.

"But she's right," Mom said. "And look, Scratchy is drinking the water after all."

Sure enough, after nosing around the water bowl, Scratchy lowered her head and began lapping up the water. Her little tongue went in and out, faster than I would have believed possible. When she was finished, she sat down right where she was and began grooming herself.

"Ooh," said Ira. "Why is she licking herself all over?"

"That's how cats clean themselves." I shot him a look to let him know how ignorant he was. "They have a patch of sharp spines that point backward right near the tip of their tongues. That helps them keep themselves clean."

"Ooh—gross!" Joey wrinkled up his freckled nose. "If I was a cat, I wouldn't want to lick up dirt and hair and all sorts of garbage from my fur! Then you'd have to swallow it!"

"If you were a cat you'd be so dirty and smelly that no one would come near you," I said. "Besides, cats' stomachs are made to handle that."

"I still think it's gross," Joey said.

But what was really gross happened a while later. Once Scratchy was done cleaning, she decided to use the litter box. And, as I had promised Mom and Dad when they agreed to let me have a kitten, I was the one responsible for cleaning it out.

I had this little "pooper scooper" I got from the pet shop. I had to dig through the litter for whatever Scratchy had made, scoop it up, and throw it in the toilet. Talk about gross—this was disgusting!

But Scratchy seemed to appreciate what I had done for her. She rubbed up against me and purred, and she allowed me to pet her without running under the bed. So it was worth a little grossness to be able to have my kitten.

Chapter
Eight

I let Scratchy stay in the house for the next few days to make sure she got used to living with me. I had her all set up in a routine that revolved around my school day.

I got up early in the morning and went straight to the bathroom. That was where my mother decided Scratchy would have to spend the night. We kept her litter box in there, and Mom didn't trust Scratchy to be far from the litter box. I wasn't too happy about this because I wanted Scratchy to sleep with me. But I didn't press the issue. I decided to wait until I could get her really well-trained. Once Mom saw what a smart cat Scratchy was, she'd see it was foolish not to let Scratchy sleep with me.

Anyhow, when I got to the bathroom, Scratchy would come up to me, meow, and rub against my legs. She was really glad to see me after spending the night alone in the bathroom, and I was glad to see her. I would pet her, which would set her off purring away.

I'd get the yucky part—emptying the litter box—over with as quickly as possible. Then I'd feed Scratchy—either some canned cat food or some of those little packages of soft stuff or just dry food from the box. In the morning, Scratchy was so hungry she would have probably eaten almost anything.

"Linda, you'd better stop playing with that cat and get ready for school," Mom would remind me each day.

"Don't worry, Ma, I've got plenty of time," I would reply. Then I would play with Scratchy some more until it was so late I'd have to race to get ready for school.

Fortunately, the end of the school year was drawing closer. I couldn't wait for school to end, couldn't wait till I had whole days to play with Scratchy and my friends. For once summer came, I had plans to have Scratchy so well-trained that I would be able to take her out in the street with me, without worrying about her running away.

In the name of science, Danny agreed to help me train Scratchy. I wanted to teach her to come to me when I called her, no matter what.

"Right after school is the best time for the training session," Danny said.

"Why is that?" I asked.

"Because she hasn't eaten since morning and should be real hot for food," he explained. "You see, we set up the situation to ask Scratchy to do something. We show her the food, but she doesn't get it until she does what we want. Then we lay on the praise and reward her with some food. Once she learns something simple, we keep making it harder for her. But we always use the same technique—she only gets food when she does it right. That's positive reinforcement."

"Oh." I was impressed. Sometimes it pays off to have a "brain" like Danny for a friend.

We started off with something real easy. Danny took Scratchy to one end of the room. I stood at the other end with some dry cat food and held it out to her. "Here, Scratchy. Here, girl," I called.

Scratchy saw the food and ran to me right away. "Good girl! You did it!" I patted her happily and let her eat the food from my hand. "You see, Danny, what a smart cat she is? She came the very first time!" I said proudly.

"That's no big deal. I expected her to do that— the food was practically in front of her nose," he said. "The tough part comes later on—when you put obstacles in her way so she has to get around them to get to you. Then you make it even harder so she can hear you but can't see you. Then you do both—put obstacles in her way and go where she can't see you. If she comes then, that's when she's really trained."

"That's boring," Ira said, poking his head into the room.

"When are you going to teach her real tricks?

Neat stuff like rolling over and shaking hands, or fetching a ball like dogs do," asked Joey, who was right behind Ira.

"Cats don't do tricks like that," I told them.

"Well, why not?" said Ira.

"'Cause—'cause—" I really didn't know the reason.

"'Cause cats are dumber than dogs." Ira smiled triumphantly.

"No. Because no one ever bothers to train them to do tricks," Danny broke in. "There's no reason you can't teach a cat tricks if you work at it."

"I bet you can't teach Scratchy," said Joey. "She's too wild and dumb."

"I bet we can," I said back.

"Give us one month with this kitten," said Danny. "We'll have her doing all sorts of tricks."

"It's a bet," both my brothers said together in what seemed like stereophonic sound.

"Loser buys the winners an ice-cream soda," Ira said.

"That's how sure we are we're going to win," said Joey.

"What about me?" asked Danny. "I'm in this, too."

"I'll tell you what, Danny," I said. "If you help me train Scratchy so I can win this contest, I'll buy you a double banana split!"

After one week, Scratchy's training was coming along well, but not as well as I would have liked it.

With a lot of effort, Danny and I got Scratchy to come when I called her, even when I was in another room. But somehow, she couldn't seem to get the hang of rolling over or shaking hands.

"We told you only dogs were smart enough to learn tricks like that," said Joey. He and Ira laughed at the sight of Danny and me down on our knees trying to show Scratchy what we expected of her when we said, "roll over."

"Get lost, brats!" I scrambled to my feet and chased them out of the bedroom. The last people I needed to have around when things weren't going well with Scratchy were my brothers.

Ira and Joey ran straight to the kitchen to tattle on me to Mommy. "Ma! Linda called us brats in front of Danny!" Joey called.

"Linda, please don't call your brothers names," Mom's exasperated voice rang out. "Remember, it's their room as well as yours."

Ira and Joey returned and stuck their tongues out at me. "See, Ma said it's our room, too," said Ira.

"And you have no right to kick us out of it," said Joey. They plopped themselves down on their beds to watch what Danny and I were doing.

I made up my mind to ignore my brothers and concentrate on Scratchy. Truthfully, Danny and I weren't quite sure about the best way to teach her to roll over. We tried ordering her to do it while we flipped her body with our hands. That was fine as long as we kept flipping, but we couldn't get her to do it on her own.

Then we got the idea of showing her what we wanted her to do. Danny said, "Roll over," making the sign for it with his hand. I rolled over. Then Danny made a big fuss over me, patting my head and pretending to give me some cat food.

Scratchy came prancing over and tried to get some cat food for herself. But she still couldn't seem to make the connection between rolling over and getting the cat food.

Then Danny came up with a brainstorm. "How about if we make it easy for her by getting her to just roll over halfway? Put her on her back, tell her to roll over, and see if she'll scramble to her feet." He began positioning Scratchy as he spoke.

"Look! She did it! She did it!" I called excitedly as Scratchy stood up quickly.

"Big deal!" Joey scoffed.

"She'd get up off her back whether you said 'roll over' or 'brush your teeth,'" added Ira.

I had to admit my brothers were probably right. I sat down next to Scratchy and began rubbing her between the ears the way she liked it. "We've got to think of some other way to teach her this trick."

"There is no other way," said Ira.

"We told you—she's just a dumb kitten. She can't learn hard tricks like dogs can," said Joey.

"Why don't you just get out of here, brats?" I snapped. "Go back to the kitchen and get another snack or something."

"Good idea." My brothers, who are always hungry, bounded out of the room.

"Finally. Some peace and quiet," I said to Danny. "You don't know how lucky you are to be an only child."

"Hanging around with you and your brothers never fails to convince me," he said with a grin. "But seriously, I think we've got to come up with a different reward for Scratchy. I don't think this dry cat food interests her enough for her to do something difficult."

"You're probably right," I said grimly. "But I don't know what else to try with her. She likes canned cat food better, but Mom would kill me if I ever took it out of the kitchen. That stuff smells so bad that it's hard enough getting it out of the can and into the bowl, without suffocating. If it ever got on anything else, like the rug, the smell would probably never go away."

"That's why your cat smells so awful, too!" The twins returned and plopped themselves down on Ira's bed. They were carrying a large bowl of Cheese Doodles, which they then placed between them. They began munching away, not even caring that they were getting crumbs all over. Mom would have killed them if she knew.

I was about to come back with a fitting reply when Danny grabbed my arm. "Don't even bother answering them, Linda. If you're going to fight with your brothers all day, we'll never get anything accomplished with Scratchy."

But Scratchy had some ideas of her own. She squirmed away from me and leaped right up on

Ira's bed. She began licking up the crumbs my brothers had dropped on the bedspread. When she finished those, she headed for the bowl.

My brothers saw what Scratchy had in mind and got up fast. "Get your cat away from us! She's trying to eat our Cheese Doodles," Ira said. Joey shoved Scratchy off the bed.

But Scratchy didn't give up so easily. As soon as she hit the floor, she hopped back up on the bed again and headed for the Cheese Doodles.

"Linda!" Ira shrieked. "Get that cat out of here!"

"Okay, okay." I laughed as I removed Scratchy from the bed. "Boy, she really goes for those Cheese Doodles."

"Cheese Doodles! That's it!" Danny got up from the floor excitedly. "Here, Ira. Let me have one of those."

"What for?" Ira asked. But Danny was already holding a Cheese Doodle out to Scratchy. She eyed it carefully as he moved it in a circular motion.

"Come on, Scratchy. Roll over—like this!" Danny pushed her on one side. She bounded to her feet and tried to get the Cheese Doodles.

"Oh, no. That's not good enough," said Danny. "Come on, now. ROLL OVER!" He moved the Cheese Doodle in a circle again, and I couldn't believe what happened next: Scratchy rolled over the way we'd been trying to get her to do for days!

"Good girl!" Danny gave her the Cheese Doodle and patted her on the head. He smiled at me in triumph. "See what a little science will do?"

"And our Cheese Doodles," Joey said glumly. "Linda, if you win this bet with our food, it doesn't count. We're not buying you the ice-cream soda!"

"Oh, who cares about the ice-cream soda, anyway?" I said. And I meant it. What really mattered was that Scratchy was finally getting trained, and that meant I would be able to take her outside.

Chapter Nine

That Saturday, I decided that Scratchy was ready. I was going to take her outside with me for the first time since I had brought her home.

Danny was sure that Scratchy was trained well enough to make it on her own. But I didn't feel as secure as he did. After all, what did he have to lose if Scratchy ran away? She was my cat, not Danny's.

"I'm going to rig up a leash for her." I held out a piece of rope to which I had fastened a large safety pin. "The pin hooks on to Scratchy's collar so I can walk her like a dog."

"Boy, that looks dumb," was Danny's comment.

"Well, maybe I won't need it after a while," I said. "But this is her very first time out."

I held Scratchy in my arms until we were out in the courtyard. Billy and Teddy were already there, tossing a ball back and forth.

"Hey, what took you guys so long to get out this

morning?" Billy asked. "It seems like we've been waiting for you forever."

"That's because we had to get Scratchy ready," I said, holding out my arms so they could see her.

Billy and Teddy stopped tossing the ball and came over to look at Scratchy. She was huddled up against me, her eyes big and wide, taking in the sights of her new environment.

"Hey, Scratchy!" Teddy patted her head. "How've you been, girl? We sure miss you and Smokey and Tiger around my house these days."

"How are Smokey and Tiger doing in their new homes, anyway?" I asked.

"Well, Smokey's doing fine living with my cousin Loretta—I don't think you ever met her, Linda. As for Tiger—well, what would you expect from a jerk like my cousin Raymond? He'd only had Tiger for three days when he started mistreating him. Raymond never remembered to feed Tiger or change his litter box. When Tiger would cry, Raymond just kicked him. So Raymond's mother decided Tiger had to go."

"Go? Go where?" I asked. "Are you taking Tiger back to your house, Teddy?"

"Nope." Teddy shook his head. "I wish I could, but I can't. Mom says one cat's more than enough to deal with when you're making a big move—like to Long Island."

"Long Island? Who's moving to Long Island?" asked Danny.

"We are." Teddy kicked the ball up against the courtyard wall.

For a moment, we all stood there, just watching as the ball bounced back to him again. It was hard to believe what Teddy had said. Move to Long Island!

"You're just kidding us, right?" Billy asked.

"I wish I was." Teddy shook his head. "But Mom and Dad broke the news to us last night. They decided they can't take living in the city any longer. They found a house they liked way out on Long Island. We're going to be moving at the end of the summer so we can be settled in by the time school starts."

"Oh, Teddy, that's awful!" I said. "How are we ever going to get a good ballgame going without you? And Tiger—what's going to happen to him?"

"Well, my aunt tried to find someone to take him," said Teddy. "But no one she knew wanted a cat. So she called up the ASPCA to come and get him."

"What's the ASPCA?" asked Billy.

"It's the American Society for Prevention of Cruelty to Animals," I told him. "They pick up stray dogs and cats and animals people don't want. Then they try to find them good homes."

"But you know what happens if they can't find a home for the animals, don't you?" said Danny. "They do away with them."

"Do away with them?" I was horrified at the thought. "You can't mean that, Danny! Why would they do away with dogs and cats?"

"Because they don't have enough room for all of them. So if no one wants an animal after a certain amount of time, they have to get rid of them. It's called 'putting them to sleep'—forever!"

"That's awful!" I exclaimed. I turned to Teddy. "Oh, Teddy, do you think they'll put poor little Tiger to sleep?"

"No," he said. "Tiger is a young cat and really cute. They told us they were sure he'd get adopted fast."

"But you don't even know what kind of people might adopt him. Oh! I've got to do something about this! Hang on to Scratchy for me, Danny." I handed him the rope. "I'm going to go talk to my mother!"

"I see your mom said no," Danny commented when I came back down to the courtyard a few minutes later.

"Yeah," I said glumly. "Mom said that one cat is more than enough for our family and that if we went around trying to adopt every animal brought to the ASPCA, there soon wouldn't be enough room for us in the apartment at all." I shook my head. "But I wasn't asking for every animal—just Tiger!"

"Well, be happy you've got Scratchy," said Teddy. "If you hadn't picked her she might have wound up at the ASPCA, too."

"I am happy I have Scratchy." I picked her up and hugged her. Her fur was so soft, and she smelled so good outside in the hot June sun. "How's she been outside while I was gone, Danny?"

"Great!" he said. "She's already explored the whole courtyard. I let go of her rope, but she always comes right back to me when I call her."

"You let go of her rope? Danny! How could you? What if she'd run out into the street?" Clutching Scratchy, I sat down on the stoop.

"Oh, she wouldn't have—I was fully prepared for any emergencies." Danny reached down into his pants' pocket and pulled out a small bag of Cheese Doodles.

As soon as Scratchy saw them, she squirmed out of my arms. She went running over to Danny, meowing as if she hadn't eaten in weeks. Boy, did that cat love Cheese Doodles!

The rest of Scratchy's "outing" went well. Danny and I walked all the way up the block with her. At first, I held tightly to her rope, but it seemed she was perfectly happy to follow me and the Cheese Doodles wherever we might go. So, on the way back, I unpinned the rope and let Scratchy walk behind me on her own.

She was having a great time! She sniffed around the sidewalk, stopping to look at all sorts of amazing things like fire hydrants and car tires and ants crawling by. And whenever she would start to dawdle, I would call, "Here Scratchy, here girl," and she would come running. Then I would give her a Cheese Doodle and pat her head and tell her how wonderful she was.

On Sunday, I took Scratchy out again. This time I didn't even bother hooking up the rope. I just brought it along in case of an emergency. I brought a full bag of Cheese Doodles, too. Then I let Scratchy walk on the street tagging along after me.

It was a lot of fun. People I didn't even know would stop and comment about Scratchy and how cute she was following me along the street. If it was someone I did know, I would pick Scratchy up and hold her so she could be petted. Scratchy was getting a lot of attention, and so was I.

I ran into Teddy coming out of his building, and he started to walk along with Scratchy and me. "It looks as if we'll be moving to Long Island sooner than I expected," he told me. "The house we're buying is empty, and the people are anxious to close the deal. Dad says it looks like we'll be out in early August."

"Oh, Teddy! That hardly gives you any time here!"

"I know. And if I had my choice we wouldn't move at all. It's funny, because at one time I thought it would be great to move to a house. I'd have my own room and all that. But now that I'm leaving, I can see that having a room isn't what's really important. It's having friends that matters. I don't know anyone in Long Island. I'm sure going to miss you and Danny, and Scratchy, too."

I was so engrossed in what Teddy was telling me that I took my eyes off Scratchy. It was only for a moment, but it was enough time for this huge, mean-looking alley cat to rush out from between two parked cars and head straight for her.

"Watch out for that big tom!" called Teddy. But it was too late. The cat had already reached Scratchy.

I couldn't believe what happened next: Scratchy drew her back up into a big arch and puffed up her fur so she was twice her normal size. She began making these awful hissing and growling sounds. I had never seen anything like it.

I don't think the tom had either. He stopped short in his tracks and stood there staring at Scratchy with his evil-looking eyes. You could tell this tom had been in plenty of fights: His fur was all battered and torn; he had scabbed-over scratches on his nose; and one yellow eye drooped way down.

I don't know if he wanted to fight with Scratchy or not, but I wasn't going to take any chances. Quickly, I jumped between the two hissing cats. I scooped Scratchy up in my arms and ran down the block, with her still bristling and howling.

"There, Scratchy. It's all right, girl," I kept saying as I patted her between her ears, trying to calm her down and myself, too. She was so frightened I could hear her heart hammering.

"Is Scratchy okay?" asked Teddy, coming down the block after me.

I just nodded. I was too upset to even talk. Scratchy had come to mean so much to me. What would I do if anything ever happened to her?

Chapter Ten

Summer vacation finally arrived, and it was wonderful to have my cat to spend it with. Each day, I took Scratchy out with me on her rope leash. Each night, while I read books or watched TV, Scratchy would curl up next to me. She would purr while I stroked her warm, soft fur.

With Scratchy there beside me I was never bored. I was never lonely. If something bothered me, I would talk to her about it. Of course, she couldn't answer me, but she would look at me as if she really did understand. She would nuzzle her head against me and lick my hand. No matter what, Scratchy made me feel good.

I knew that Scratchy was the best pet there ever was. I wanted the whole world to know it. On the Fourth of July, I finally got my chance.

Each year, the recreation department of the park near our house held a party for the neighborhood on the Fourth of July. There was a picnic in the park, complete with a band, a bicycle parade, and a pet contest. There were awards for the best-looking, the smartest, the cutest, the funniest, and the ugliest pets. I was sure Scratchy would have no trouble winning in any of the categories—except the ugliest, of course.

The pet contest was the morning's first event. All pets had to be signed up for entry before nine-thirty. I got Scratchy ready bright and early, giving her a bath and brushing her coat until it shone. I tried tying a red ribbon around her neck to make her look even prettier, but she kept chewing it off. I decided the judges would just have to recognize her beauty in its unadorned state.

I was all set to go. Since I had to be at the park early to enter Scratchy in the contest, the plan was that my parents and brothers would meet me there later. They would bring a picnic lunch, and we would spend the day there, watching the contests and listening to the band. But these arrangements were not good enough for my brothers. As soon as they saw I was ready, they began their demands.

"Make Linda take us with her, Ma. We don't want to wait for you," said Ira.

"We want to see the pet contest, too. We want to go now!" added Joey.

My mother probably would have stuck me with my brothers, but I came up with the perfect excuse: "I can't take them this time, Ma. I'm going to be busy with Scratchy and the contest. I won't be able to watch her and Ira and Joey at the same time. The park will be jammed with people. It'll be dangerous for them."

This was something my mother could relate to. There was no way she would allow her precious twins to be put in a dangerous situation. For once, she saw it my way. She told Ira and Joey they would have to wait for her and my father to get ready. She promised to get them to the park in time to see the pet contest.

I grabbed Scratchy, her leash, and a bag of Cheese Doodles. I headed for the door before my brothers could come up with any other angles for getting me to take them along.

"Wait a minute!" My mother stopped me. "You can't take Scratchy to the park with just a leash. You've got to take her in the cat-carrier."

"The cat-carrier! But Ma, I hate that contraption. Scratchy is used to going out with me on a leash."

"That's fine for around the block," my mother said. "But the park's too far, and you have to cross a big street to get there. Scratchy could get loose and you both could get hit by a car."

I had to admit my mother had a point. So I went to the closet and got down the carton Danny had made into a cat-carrier. Scratchy protested loudly as I put her in it. She climbed out three times before I finally got it shut and we were ready to go.

I was glad I had Scratchy in the cat-carrier when I ran into Brenda Roman in the elevator. Brenda was holding Pretty Boy in his cage, which was all decorated with red, white, and blue ribbons. As soon as that parrot saw me he began squawking. "Pretty Boy! Pretty Boy! *Awk, awk, aawkk!*" The sound was so ear-splitting I couldn't stand it.

"Can't you do something to quiet that bird down?" I put the hand that wasn't holding the cat-carrier over one ear.

"Quiet, Pretty Boy," Brenda said, but Pretty Boy kept squawking away. Brenda turned to me and shrugged. "I guess he's all excited. I'm taking him to the park to enter him in the Fourth of July pet contest. He's so gorgeous, he's bound to win. Aren't you, Pretty Boy?" She put her face right up against the cage and began clucking at him.

"Pretty Boy loves you. Pretty Boy loves you! *Awk—aawwkkk!*" The parrot shrieked.

I was hoping he'd nip into Brenda's cheek, but no such luck. "Why don't you cover his cage or something so maybe he'll shut up?"

"I can't do that—it might mess up his ribbons!" Brenda stuck her tongue out at me.

I would have punched her, but I was carrying Scratchy. And the elevator door opened so I was able to get away from Brenda and her squawking parrot.

"Don't be so sure about Pretty Boy's winning anything, Brenda," I warned her. "When the judges see my cat, Scratchy, no other pet will stand a chance!"

The noise level at the pet show was so loud it made Pretty Boy's squawking seem like nothing.

67

Half the neighborhood kids seemed to have brought pets with them. The sound of all the dogs barking, cats meowing, and birds screeching was deafening.

As soon as we were safely in the park, I put the cat-carrier down and let Scratchy out of it. I attached the rope-leash to her collar, but she seemed a bit nervous so I picked her up and held her. Good thing I did that, too. Because a moment later, a big dog came bounding up to us. Scratchy clung to me in fear.

"Somebody get that monster away from my cat!" I yelled.

"Winston is not a monster. He's an Irish wolf-hound," someone yelled back. I looked and saw it was Matthew Bainbridge struggling to hold on to the end of the dog's leash.

Matthew had been in my class at school last year. He had dark curly hair and big brown eyes, and he played a good game of ball. I had always thought he was pretty nice and pretty cute. But right now I wasn't happy to see him or his dog.

"I don't care what he is—get him away from my cat!" I held Scratchy protectively.

"He just wants to be friends," Matthew said. "Winston likes cats, see?"

As if to prove Matthew right, Winston stood on his hind legs. He placed his massive paws on my shoulders and began to lick Scratchy's fur with his huge tongue. I could picture him biting her little head off!

"Get him off of me!" I yelled again. I twisted my body in an attempt to get away from Winston.

My attempt didn't work. With Winston's weight on my shoulders, I lost my balance and went sprawling to the ground. Winston, probably thinking this was some sort of new game, came bounding on top of me. He joyously licked my face and drooled on me the whole time.

Yuck! It was disgusting, having dog drool all over me. And the sight of Matthew's laughing face as he pretended to pull Winston away from me made me absolutely furious.

I guess I shouldn't have done what I did next. But I was so angry, I couldn't think straight. Holding Scratchy with one hand, I reached down with the other and grabbed a fistful of dirt.

"Take that!" I threw the dirt at Matthew. He ducked and lost his grip on Winston's leash, and at the same time Scratchy managed to squirm away from me. She let out a meow and raced away. Winston took off after her, barking like crazy.

"Scratchy! Come back!" I called, scrambling to my feet. But Scratchy paid no attention. She and Winston were already heading to the back part of the park, where there was a field surrounded by clumps of trees and bushes.

Matthew stood there wiping the dirt from his face. I grabbed his wrist. "Come on," I said. "We've got to get them before they get lost for good."

We ran as fast as we could, but by the time we

reached the field, Scratchy and Winston had already disappeared. We stopped and looked around unsure of which way to go. Then we heard an outbreak of barking and meowing that was coming from a large cluster of trees and bushes.

"There—to the left!" Matthew said excitedly. We both plunged off through the bushes.

I had scraped my left knee and right elbow by the time we found them. Winston was barking away under this large maple tree, and there, out on a high branch, was Scratchy.

"Scratchy! Don't worry! I'll get you down!" I called with more confidence than I felt, because the branch she was on was a good six feet over my head. Even the lowest branches were too high to reach. What was I going to do?

"I could boost you up so you could reach the lowest branch," Matthew said, as if he were reading my mind.

I looked at him in surprise. Matthew didn't look angry anymore. In fact, he was smiling as if he wanted to be friends. Well, why shouldn't he anyhow? His pet was safe and sound. It was mine that was stuck up in the tree.

This thought made me madder than ever, so mad that I couldn't help but wonder how I had ever thought Matthew was the slightest bit cute. He certainly didn't look cute now, with dirt smeared all over his face! I was about to give him a fitting wise-guy answer, but, fortunately, I managed to keep quiet. Because right now the fact remained that I needed Matthew to help me climb the tree.

So I waited while Matthew tied Winston to a tree far away from Scratchy's. Then I obediently followed his directions.

He bent down and told me to climb to his shoulders and wrap my arms around his head. Once I was sitting up there, he slowly straightened up.

"Hurry up and get off me. You're heavy!" he exclaimed.

I was scared stiff to let go of his head, but I could hear Scratchy meowing with fright. That gave me the courage to reach out and grab for the lowest branch of the tree. Once I had that, I pulled myself up onto the branch into the tree and sat there, holding on to it.

"You're up there!" He announced it as if this was news to me. "Can you reach Scratchy?"

"I don't think so." Gingerly, I stood up on my branch and reached upward. I still couldn't get to Scratchy.

"Then climb up higher!"

I had to climb up two more levels before I finally got to Scratchy's branch. And then I had to stretch way out to reach her, because she was all the way at the end of the branch. To make matters worse, Scratchy was so frightened she dug her claws into the bark and wouldn't let go.

I could see why, too. From the ground the branch had not seemed to be too high up, but now that I was up there, looking down, the distance seemed much greater. I was scared. But I wasn't going to show it in front of Matthew.

"Come on, Scratchy, come on," I pleaded with her. "I'm here to help you." I struggled to pry her loose and still keep my grip on the tree, but it was of no use. I couldn't get Scratchy to budge.

"Maybe if you bribe her—with some food or something," Matthew suggested.

"Food? That's it! Why didn't I think of that before?" I felt hope beginning to surge through me. "Matthew, do me a favor. Go back to the front of the park where I left Scratchy's cat-carrier. There's a bag of Cheese Doodles inside. Get it and bring it to me, will you?"

"Cheese Doodles? What for?"

"Please, Matthew! There's no time for explanations. Just get it for me, okay?"

"Okay." Matthew ran off with Winston to get the bag. When he came back, he tossed it up to where I was waiting in the tree. I caught the bag and quickly got out some Cheese Doodles. I threw the bag back down to Matthew and held the Cheese Doodles in my hand to Scratchy.

"Here, Scratchy. Here, girl." At the sound of the familiar call, Scratchy's ears twitched. Her nose began twitching, too. I held tightly to the branch with one hand and prayed silently. Please, please, let Scratchy come for the Cheese Doodles.

"Meow!" Scratchy began inching slowly toward me.

"Good girl!" I let her eat the Cheese Doodles from my hand. When they were finished, I grabbed her and tucked her under my arm where she held on to me for dear life. Then slowly, painfully, I started backing down the tree.

When I made it to the lowest branch, I lowered Scratchy to where Matthew could grab on to her. Then I held on to the branch with both my hands, swung from it briefly, and dropped to the ground.

"Here's your dumb old cat." Matthew held Scratchy out to me. I took her in my arms and nestled my face into the soft white part of her fur.

"Oh, Scratchy," I whispered. "If anything had happened to you, I don't know what I would have done. You're the best thing that ever happened to me."

I was so engrossed in Scratchy, that for a moment I forgot that Matthew was standing there listening to all the mushy things I was saying. I could have died of embarrassment when I heard him say, "Well, if that's the way you feel, you really ought to get her entered in the pet contest. So let's get moving—it's probably close to nine-thirty by now!"

It was more than close to nine-thirty. It was nine-forty by the time we got back to the registration desk. We were too late, Matthew and I, so neither Winston nor Scratchy could be entered in the contest.

Matthew and I sat there watching the other pets

parade by the judges' stand. By that time, Winston and Scratchy were so used to each other, it was as if they were old friends.

It was disgusting to watch this fat German Shepherd that wasn't half as classy as Winston win the ribbon for best dog. And to see some white Angora, dressed in a little dress and wheeled around in a doll carriage, win the prize for prettiest cat. But what really got to me was seeing Brenda Roman's face when Pretty Boy took first prize in the bird category. Couldn't the judges tell a low-class parrot when they saw one?

It was probably just as well I didn't get Scratchy signed up for the contest. Chances were the judges wouldn't have recognized her greatness, anyhow. But I did. And to make sure Scratchy knew it, I braided her a green ribbon out of blades of grass I picked and looped it through her collar.

She chewed it off right away—which she would have done even if it was a blue ribbon. And what did some stupid old ribbon mean, anyway? I knew Scratchy was the best cat ever, and that was what counted.

What also counted was that Scratchy and I had a great time spending most of the day with Winston and Matthew. We went from his parents' picnic blanket to mine, picking up snacks for ourselves and Winston and Scratchy. We watched the bicycles, all decked out in colored streamers and balloons, parade by. We listened to the band play patriotic songs.

Matthew told me I wouldn't be seeing him around next school year because he and his family had moved across the George Washington Bridge to Fort Lee, New Jersey. They had bought a house with a big yard for Winston to run in. Since Matthew didn't have any brothers or sisters, he was hoping to get another pet.

"At first I thought I'd like another dog," Matthew said. "But now that I've met Scratchy and seen how much fun she is, I think I'll look for a cat just like her."

"There will never be another cat as smart and wonderful as Scratchy," I said, nuzzling up to her.

As if to prove my point, Scratchy meowed and licked my face. I rewarded her by giving her a piece of the tuna-fish sandwich my mother had insisted I take on my last stop at our picnic blanket. Scratchy gobbled it up, bread and all, as if she were starved.

Matthew and I both laughed to see her. Little did I know then that Scratchy's new-found eating habits were about to cause so much trouble.

Chapter Eleven

It was at the picnic that Scratchy came to appreciate the joys of eating people food. After that, she began hanging around under the table at mealtimes, in the hopes that someone would drop something to the floor that was good to eat. If that happened, she would rush over, sniff it, and, if it met with her approval, she would eat it up.

My mother was not too fond of having Scratchy under the table at mealtimes. But I convinced her that Scratchy actually made cleaning up so much easier. It was almost like having a miniature vacuum cleaner there, ready to spring into action. Because of Scratchy, the kitchen floor was always clean.

Of course, I didn't tell my mother I had begun feeding extra tidbits to Scratchy, in addition to the food which fell on the floor. Sometimes she would stand by my chair, looking at me with pleading eyes. I couldn't resist slipping her something I knew she would like. Or sometimes I would be eating something I didn't like, and I was only too glad to share it with her.

No matter what I gave her, Scratchy seemed to like it. It was getting so she liked people food better than cat food. I thought this was really cute.

Unfortunately, Scratchy's love for people food began creating problems. It didn't take her long to realize that the table was where the food action took place in our house. Once she knew this, it was only natural for her to hop up there to investigate what was happening.

My mother didn't appreciate this at all. "Linda!" she called in horror the first time she caught Scratchy on the table. "Get that cat off the table this instant. And if you know what's good for you, you'll see she never comes up here again!"

By the time I got into the kitchen, Scratchy had already jumped off the table. She scooted by me and raced down the hallway into my room. I ran after her and found her huddled under my bed.

"Scratchy! You come out right now!" I demanded as I peered under the bed.

Of course she wouldn't. She knew she had done something wrong. I had to crawl under the bed and pull her out.

"Scratchy!" I looked into her eyes and said, "This is serious! Mom is big on cleanliness to begin with, but when it comes to food she's absolutely insane. You've got to keep off the table. You've got to! Do you hear me?"

Scratchy meowed and rubbed her little head against me as if she had done nothing wrong. She rolled on her back so I could rub her belly.

I sighed. Scratchy looked so cute I couldn't resist petting her. "Look, Scratchy. This better not happen again. Understand?"

"Meow," said Scratchy.

All I could do was hope she'd keep off the table and that Mom wouldn't catch her if she didn't.

The next person to find Scratchy on the table had to be my brother Joey. If it had been Ira, there would have been a chance he wouldn't have made a big deal about it. But Joey was the nastier of the two by far. He had to play the incident for all it was worth.

"Ma! Come here and look at Linda's cat. She's on the table trying to get into the butter dish!"

You would have thought the kitchen was on fire or something the way my mother came flying in. "Get off of there!" she screamed at Scratchy.

Ira and I ran into the kitchen in time to see Scratchy oblige. She jumped to the floor and tried to hide behind the legs of a chair.

"Get out of here! Get!" my mother kept yelling. Then she took a broom and chased after Scratchy with it. "Don't you ever get on my kitchen table again!"

Poor Scratchy was terrified. She tried to get away from my mother by weaving her way through the maze of table-and-chair legs. My mother kept swatting at her with the broom.

Finally, when Scratchy had run out of hiding places, she took a desperate leap from the floor to the washing machine. That's where my mother kept her favorite gardenia plant so it could catch the rays of the morning sun.

Crash! The plant went flying to the floor. The pot shattered, and dirt, leaves, and crushed gardenia blossoms filled the air.

"Meow*rl!*" Scratchy went scampering out of the room.

"Get her! Get her!" Joey yelled.

"Oooh! Look what a mess she made!" Ira pointed it out, as if my mother didn't already know.

"My prize gardenia. It took me years to get it to bloom!" My mother gazed at what was left of her plant as if she were in shock. She went over to a flower that had survived mostly intact and fingered a damaged petal. "I can't believe it. It was so beautiful until it was ruined by that—that ANIMAL!"

She turned to look at me where I stood frozen in the entranceway to the kitchen. "Linda! You'd better do something to discipline that cat and make sure nothing like this ever happens again. This is her last chance. One more problem like this and you'll have to find another home for her. Do you understand?"

"Sure, Ma. It won't happen again. I promise," I

79

told her. But I didn't feel comfortable with the situation. I could make a promise for myself and stick to it all right. But how could I get a cat to stick to a promise?

That night, when Dad came home from work, Mom lost no time in reporting all the damage done by Scratchy. They went into their room together and were in there a long time.

When they came out, Dad looked at me and sighed. "Well, Linda. How about you and I taking a little walk together after dinner tonight?"

I knew this meant trouble. When I was little, Dad and I used to take all sorts of walks together. We would go up to Fort Tryon Park, the big park about a mile from my house. We would walk across the George Washington Bridge to New Jersey. Those kind of walks were always fun.

But the kind of walk Dad had in mind now was totally different. He was referring to what I called a "walk and talk." That meant the walk was an excuse to give me a talking-to. Chances were the talking-to was something I had no desire to hear.

I wasn't wrong. Oh, Dad was nice about it. He softened me up first by buying me a huge strawberry-ice-cream cone. It was a good thing I had finished the ice-cream cone by the time he got down to what he wanted to say. I probably wouldn't have been able to eat it after that.

"Your mother and I have decided it would be a

good experience for you to go to sleep-away camp for part of the summer." Dad lost no time getting down to the issue. We were sitting on a bench in the back of the park, and I was wiping my sticky fingers off on a napkin.

"Sleep-away camp? Whatever for?" I asked, puzzled. "I like it fine here in the city in the summer."

"Maybe so," said Dad. "But I'm sure you could benefit from a camp experience. You'd meet girls and boys your age, get to play ball and go swimming, do arts and crafts, and find out what it's like to be away from home. It would be good for you."

"Good for me doesn't mean I'd like it," I said suspiciously. "Besides, isn't it too late in the summer for me to get in to camp?"

"Ordinarily, it would be," Dad said. "But it so happens that Brenda Roman's mother has some pull at Camp Winnepeg because Brenda's been going there since she was six years old. When your mother told her recently we would like to send you to camp, Mrs. Roman was nice enough to speak to the director on your behalf. Well, this afternoon the camp called to say a spot opened up. It's for the three-week session starting in late July. That's the same session Brenda will be going to, so you'll already have a friend."

"Friend?" I gasped. "Brenda and I could never be friends. She's the last person on earth I'd want to go to camp with."

"I'm sorry you feel that way about Brenda. But

that doesn't change the fact that it'll be good for you to go to camp. Especially with all that's been going on with Scratchy."

"Scratchy? What's camp got to do with Scratchy? Except for the fact that I obviously can't go away because I have to be here to take care of her."

"No, you don't. The rest of us can manage to take care of her while you're gone. That is, providing she starts behaving herself. Truthfully, I have to tell you that was another thing your mother and I discussed, Linda. If that cat continues jumping on the table and getting into our food, we won't be able to keep her any longer. We probably should get rid of her now, before she causes any more damage. But since we know how much you love the cat, we decided to use the time left before you go to camp as a trial."

"Trial? What kind of trial?" I was getting more and more upset as I listened to my father.

"A trial to see if you can train her properly or not. If you can, we'll be happy to care for her while you're away at camp."

"And if I can't?"

"You have until you leave to find a good home for her. I'm sure you remember that when I first told you that you could have a cat, I also said we'd have to see how it worked out, Linda. Well, if the cat goes on the table, she's not working out. You have one more chance to shape her up, but if she can't behave she'll have to go."

I walked the rest of the way home in a daze. I

couldn't believe what Dad had just said to me. Sending me to Brenda Roman's camp when I didn't want to go was bad enough, but the thought of giving up Scratchy was too terrible to bear.

It was less than two weeks until the time I would be leaving. I had to come up with something.

Chapter Twelve

Danny. Danny was the one who could help me. Danny was smart. He would come up with something. I knew he would.

The next morning, I burst into his apartment and told him about the latest problem with Scratchy. "I need help, Danny," I said. "Either Scratchy learns to keep off the table or she's gone!"

Danny chewed on the pencil he had been working with. It didn't matter that it was summer vacation. Danny was always doing some math problem.

"Gone?" he asked. "Do you think your parents really mean that, Linda? Maybe they're bluffing."

"I don't think so. You know how nutty my mother is when it comes to food. Everything has to be fresh, and everything has to be clean. In her mind, cleanliness and cats don't go together. To make matters worse, my parents are sending me away to camp. If I can't get Scratchy to behave by then, I won't even be here to defend her."

"Hmm. This sounds more serious than I thought." Danny stroked his chin. "Obviously, what's called for here is a little scientific concentration. How about if we put up a gate by the kitchen door so she can't get in?"

"That might work if she were a dog," I said. "But cats are great climbers. Anything high enough to keep her out would keep us out as well."

"Then how about barricading Scratchy in somewhere where she can't get out? Somewhere like the bathroom."

"No good. She'd cry and howl if she were stuck in the bathroom all day. Mom would never stand for the noise."

"Well, then the only thing left is trying to train her to stay off the table."

"That's exactly why I came to you. But how do we go about doing it?"

"Negative reinforcement," Danny said proudly.

"Negative reinforcement? What's that?"

"The reverse of positive reinforcement. What we do is give Scratchy some sort of adverse stimulation every time she approaches the table. Eventually, she'll come to associate it with something bad, instead of with good food. Once that happens she'll know to keep away."

"Sounds good. Now what exactly is this adverse stimulation?"

"Oh, anything that's unpleasant. How about a minor electric shock? We could run the wires to her collar and—"

"Danny! I'm not going to give Scratchy an electric shock!"

"Well, I don't see what else you can do." He shrugged. "Unless you want to stand by the table all day so you can yell at her whenever she comes too close. That'll work too, you know. But you're going to get awfully tired of standing by the kitchen table."

"I don't care," I said firmly. "Scratchy's worth it. Besides, I don't have to stand. I can sit and read and—"

"Wait a minute!" Danny interrupted me." Maybe there is another way! We can set up a situation where Scratchy gets rewarded for staying off the table and eating from her bowl."

"Sounds great!" I perked up. "How?"

"Well, let's see." Danny scratched his head thoughtfully. "What if we take her favorite food— is it still Cheese Doodles?"

I nodded.

"Good. That makes it easy. Well, there's no point in explaining it all to you now. Come downstairs and I'll help you set it up."

Danny really was a genius. He took some Cheese Doodles and ran a threaded needle through them. He took off the needle and knotted the thick thread so the Cheese Doodles would stay on. He placed the Cheese Doodles on the table and held on to the end of the thread, which was long enough so he could hold on to it and still stand a distance away from the table.

I put Scratchy in the middle of the floor to see what she would do. She wasted no time. She looked up at the Cheese Doodles and prepared to leap.

"No!" Danny yelled. At the same time, he jerked on the thread so the Cheese Doodles came flying off the table. This startled Scratchy so that she ran for cover under a chair.

That's when the next stage of Danny's plan went in to action. He put some Cheese Doodles into Scratchy's bowl. "Here, Scratchy," he called. "Here's where you get your food from."

Scratchy looked around suspiciously. When she felt secure that nothing else was going to come flying at her, she went over to her bowl and ate the Cheese Doodles.

"Good girl!" I went over and petted her, making a fuss, to show her she was doing the right thing. Then Danny and I repeated the process all over again.

"Do you think it's working?" I asked Danny hopefully.

"Probably. But you're going to have to repeat this a lot more times before she really understands. Personally, I don't think it's worth it. I'd rather be doing math. In fact, I was on the verge of figuring out the solution to this great problem when you interrupted me."

I sighed. I never could understand how Danny

put dumb old math problems before important real-life things like cats. But he had given me the help I needed, and that was what counted.

I worked with Scratchy all day long. By suppertime she was so full of Cheese Doodles that she had lost her appetite. She had no interest in cat food or table food. I figured it was safe for me to leave her and go out after dinner.

For the rest of the week I kept working with Scratchy. Even Ira and Joey helped me by yelling "no" at her any time she got near the table. Except for the Cheese Doodles she got as rewards, I never gave her people food at all.

Scratchy seemed to be learning what I wanted her to learn. I started to breathe a little easier. Then came the Saturday of my mother's Bridge luncheon.

Bridge was my mother's favorite card game. She was part of a group of women who got together to play every Tuesday night. Mrs. Kopler, Danny's mother, was part of the group. So was Teddy's mother, Mrs. Pappas.

But playing cards wasn't enough for the group. They decided that since they enjoyed one another's company so much, they should do other things together as well. They began meeting on one Saturday each month in addition to their card game. They would either go out for lunch at a restaurant or take turns having lunch at one another's house.

This Saturday it was my mother's turn to have the luncheon. You would think it was the major social event of the century, the way she fussed and prepared.

Plain tuna fish was good enough for my brothers and me to eat, but for some reason it wasn't good enough for the Bridge ladies. Oh, no, they had to have something called tuna mousse.

The tuna was ground up in the food processor with a lot of other ingredients, then pressed into a Jell-O mold. My mother thought it looked "just lovely," but if you asked me, I wouldn't touch the stuff.

And cheese. The same Swiss cheese I ate on perfectly good sandwiches with lettuce and tomatoes was also put through the food processor with some other stuff. Then the whole thing was poured into a fancy fluted piecrust, baked, and turned into something called a quiche.

"These are French dishes, and French cuisine is the finest in the world," Mom told me when I asked her why she was going to all this trouble.

"Then how come you don't make it for us?"

Mom sighed. "Your father doesn't appreciate fancy foods. He's definitely a meat-and-potatoes person. And somehow, I don't think you children would care for it much, either. But my Bridge friends definitely do. The others have all served beautifully when we've eaten in their houses. This is my first time having the luncheon here, and I want to make a nice impression."

The food wasn't the only thing Mom fussed about. She set the table with a tablecloth and linen napkins. She used her best china and silverware. She put fresh flowers in the center of the table. Around it, she arranged her mousse, quiche, croissant rolls, cheeses with funny names like Brie and Camembert, plus all the fancy French pastries she had gotten for dessert. Even I had to admit it looked beautiful.

Of course, I was especially careful to keep Scratchy out of the kitchen while all these preparations were being made. I kept her in the living room with me, while my brothers and I watched TV. Then my father decided to take my brothers out to the park before the ladies arrived. Since there was no one else in the house to watch Scratchy, I took her into the bathroom with me when I wanted to take a shower, and I locked the door.

At least I thought I had locked the door. But that lock is tricky. Sometimes it doesn't catch right, and it pops open when you least expect it. And that must have happened while I was singing away in the shower, totally unaware that anything was going wrong.

It wasn't until I shut the water off, wrapped my towel around me, and peered out from behind the shower curtains, that I became aware of the problem. The first thing I saw was that the door, which I thought I had locked, was open a good six inches. The next thing I saw was that Scratchy was gone!

It didn't take me long to figure out where she might have headed. Quickly, I climbed out of the tub and raced for the kitchen.

It was too late. Scratchy was already there on the beautiful tablecloth, her little tongue licking away at the tuna mousse, her back paws planted firmly in the softened Brie.

To make matters worse, the reason Scratchy had been successful in getting to the table was that my mother had left the kitchen to answer the door. She arrived back seconds after I did, followed by her group of chatting Bridge ladies. So we were all treated to the same sight at the same time.

I guess if the situation hadn't been so serious, it probably would have been funny. My mother's face was turning purple with embarrassment. The Bridge ladies looked as if they had just received the shock of their lives. I stood there, unable to move, wearing nothing but a towel and dripping water all over the kitchen floor. And, of course, there was Scratchy, watching us as if she couldn't imagine what all this fuss was about.

It didn't take long before she found out, however. "Linda! Get that cat off the table!" my mother yelled.

I didn't have to. The sound of my mother's voice must have reminded Scratchy she wasn't supposed to be on the table. Before I could do a thing, she sprang from the table, weaved her way through the legs of the startled ladies, and raced down the hallway to my room.

Clutching my towel tightly, I started after her.

"My lunch! My lunch! It's ruined! Oh, I'm so sorry, ladies. What are we going to eat now?"

I heard my mother trying to apologize to her friends. I didn't know what the big deal was—most of the food was still intact. All Mom had to do was whip up an ordinary tuna-fish salad instead of that mousse and get rid of that silly Brie, and everything else was fine. She didn't even have to throw out the mousse, either. Scratchy obviously liked it, so we could feed it to her.

I found Scratchy huddled in the corner under Ira's bed. I realized she was probably frightened by the commotion still coming from the kitchen, so I let her stay there while I dried off and put on some clothes. Then I slowly moved the bed so I could get to her, picked her up, and held her close. "It's all right, Scratchy; it's all right," I murmured softly.

But it wasn't. It was moments later that my mother came into the room. Her face was no longer purple, but it was angry.

"Linda, I'm sorry to tell you this, but I've reached the end of my tolerance. I've never been so embarrassed in my life, and it's all because of that cat. Fortunately, the women were more than understanding, and they're polite enough to eat the food she didn't get into. But I can't eat a thing. As long as that animal is in the house, I can't rest easy. I've made up my mind, so don't try to change it. You're leaving for camp on Friday. You have until then to find her another home. If you can't, I'll have to call the ASPCA and let them do it!"

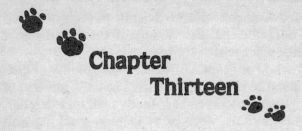

Chapter Thirteen

Call the ASPCA! I couldn't believe Mom would do that when she knew what happened to the animals they couldn't find homes for. Especially when she knew how much Scratchy meant to me.

I had been so happy since Scratchy came into my life. Even when I was stuck in the house, I was never bored or lonely. All I had to do was cuddle Scratchy and feel the softness of her fur against my face, and I would feel good again.

I was hoping that once Mom calmed down from her luncheon disaster, she would change her mind about Scratchy. It didn't happen. Every day she reminded me: "I hope you're looking for a home for that cat, Linda. Friday will be here before you know it."

I could see Mom was serious this time. She worked hard to keep our small apartment neat and to prepare us good, healthy meals. She couldn't live with a cat that got into our food, and I knew it. I decided to check with my friends to see who could take Scratchy. At least if one of them had her, I could see her whenever I wanted to.

It turned out that while there were plenty of kids who liked to pet and play with Scratchy, not one of them was able to keep her. Teddy really wanted her, but his parents were now so busy packing and getting ready to move that they refused to even consider taking another cat. Billy's father was allergic to them. Danny's mother didn't want an animal because she worked all day, and there would be no one to supervise it. Besides, Danny was worried Scratchy might get into his dumb old math papers and mess them up. I even went so far as to ask Brenda, but she was afraid a cat might hurt her precious Pretty Boy.

So, when it came down to it, there was no one to take Scratchy. I didn't know what to do besides keeping her away from Mom and the table as much as possible and praying that something would turn up.

On Thursday, the last day I had in the city before leaving for camp, I took her outside with me and found Danny, Teddy, and Billy ready to start a game of stoopball.

"Hey, Linda. You're just in time for the game," called Teddy.

"Don't you see I've got Scratchy with me," I said irritably. "I can't play ball and hold on to her at the same time."

"Aw, come on, Linda. We can't have a good game

without you. Tie the cat to a lamppost or something. She can't go anywhere, and you can watch
her while you play," said Billy.

"I don't know." I hesitated. I wanted to play, but
I wasn't sure it was a good idea to leave Scratchy
tied to the lamppost.

It was never easy to say no to Billy.

"Look, I'll show you." Billy tied Scratchy's rope-
leash to the lamppost right outside the courtyard.
The rope was long enough for her to move around,
but not long enough for her to reach the street
where she could get hit by a car. I could watch her
easily from the courtyard. And I did really want to
play ball.

"Well, I guess it would be okay." I gave in.

We started the game, and it was working out well.
Scratchy rested her head on her paws and watched
us play. Whenever the ball bounced near her, she
would get all excited and chase after it. When she
would get to the point beyond which the leash
would stretch no farther, it would jerk her to a stop.
She would shake her head and settle down until the
ball came in her direction again.

The game was a close one. We were tied four-up
in the eighth inning. Teddy was on second base, and
I was up. If I got a hit, Teddy was in a good position
to score.

I was about to take my shot when who should
come bounding out of my building but my miserable brothers. They lost no time finding some way to
annoy me.

"Look what you've done to Scratchy—tying her up that way!" Ira went to the lamppost and began patting Scratchy's head.

"Poor little thing. I bet you'll be happy when you find a new home." Joey was right there beside Ira. Anyone watching my brothers would think they really cared, but I knew perfectly well what the brats were up to.

"Just get away from Scratchy!" I yelled. They both stuck their tongues out at me and kept on petting her.

The boys began to complain. "Come on, Linda. You're holding up the game," said Billy.

"Yeah, I'm ready to make it home," said Teddy.

"All right. All right." I ignored my brothers and concentrated on taking aim. You had to hit the ball on the stoop at just the right angle. If you didn't, the ball would go wild and hit the side walls of the courtyard, which counted as an out. I lined up the ball at what I knew was the best angle and was about to throw it. Then screams from my brothers totally ruined my concentration.

"Scratchy! Scratchy's loose!" they shouted.

I looked up and stood there, too stunned to move. The lamppost was still there; the rope-leash was still there, but Scratchy wasn't. My stupid brothers! They must have untied her!

"We'll get her!" Ira and Joey were off and running.

"Don't you dare! This was all your fault!" I yelled after them. But Ira and Joey either didn't hear me or they didn't listen. By the time I got my wits together and ran out of the courtyard, they were already way down the block. Scratchy was a little speck streaking off in the distance.

Now I've had Scratchy out in the street with me loads of times, and I've even had her off her leash. She had never run off like this when she was with me. That's how I knew my brothers were to blame for this—those terrible twins who had caused me nothing but grief from the day they were born. As I ran, I didn't know which I felt most—anger at my rotten brothers or fear that something awful might happen to Scratchy.

I guess at first it was mostly anger. But when I saw Scratchy head for the gutter at the same time a car came turning onto our street, it was definitely fear that took over.

"Watch out! The car!" I screamed as loudly as I could.

I guess my brothers heard me, because they stopped short just in time. But Scratchy had disappeared into the gutter.

The car's brakes screeched, and the car came to a sudden stop. Had it stopped in time? Or was my Scratchy lying there in the street—the life crushed from her little body?

I couldn't bear to look. I covered my eyes with my hand. "Scratchy, Scratchy," I said over and over to myself, trying to force that awful picture from my mind.

"There she goes!" Danny, Billy, and Teddy ran

right by me. I looked up and saw my brothers had crossed the street ahead of the stopped car and were running up the other side of the street.

I managed to get myself going again. Scratchy had made it across the street. The car hadn't hit her. She was all right.

Or was she? Because the next turn Scratchy made was right toward the alleyway of Billy's building. And right adjoining that alleyway was a steep drop to the basement of the next building. There was a railing along the ledge, but the space underneath was high enough for a person to squeeze through. A kitten could fit through easily.

My heart beat wildly. I crossed the street and raced up the block so fast I soon caught up to Danny, Billy, and Teddy. But my brothers were way ahead of us. The two of them were lying there in the alley, stretched out on their bellies, when we found them. Ira was holding on to Joey, and Joey was holding on to something we couldn't see.

That something was Scratchy, who, sure enough, had slipped under the railing. But somehow, she had managed to grab on to the ledge with her front paws. And somehow, Joey had managed to grab on to her paws and hold them so she wouldn't slip any farther. And Ira had grabbed on to Joey so he wouldn't fall down after her.

Unfortunately, Joey didn't seem to be able to pull Scratchy back up again. "Help! Help!" he screeched. "Help me pull up this wildcat before she goes over the ledge!"

Which, of course, is what I did. With Joey holding on to Scratchy's paws, I was able to reach below the ledge and grab on to Scratchy's body. I pulled her up, got her under the railing, and hugged her to me.

Poor Scratchy was so frightened. I could feel her heart hammering inside her body. I shuddered to think of what would have happened to her if my brothers hadn't gotten to her in time. For right underneath the ledge where she had been hanging were trash cans filled with broken bottles. She never would have survived the fall if my brothers hadn't been there. If my brothers—

My brothers. I looked down to see both of them staring at me, their eyes wide with fear. Both of them had knees and elbows that were rubbed raw and bleeding from where they had scraped against the pavement. My brothers usually liked to play up each little injury as much as possible, but this time they didn't even complain.

"Is Scratchy all right?" they both asked simultaneously.

I didn't know whether to feel angry at my brothers for letting Scratchy loose or grateful to them for having saved her. So I just took a deep breath and said, "I guess so."

I turned around and began walking back to my house, ignoring everyone but Scratchy. The realization that this was to be my very last day with her suddenly hit me hard. I felt very defeated and very, very tired.

Chapter Fourteen

Mom had made an especially nice dinner that night since it was my last night at home before camp. It was turkey, stuffing, and sweet potatoes, all the things I normally loved.

I couldn't eat it. I was too aware that this was not only my last night but also Scratchy's last night as well. I had not been able to find a home for Scratchy. Tomorrow, when I left for camp, my mother would take her to the ASPCA. She would be lost to me forever.

I pushed my food around on my plate, trying to make it look like I had eaten something. I didn't say a word to anyone.

For a change, my mother didn't nag me to finish everything on my plate. She seemed to sense that this was a difficult time for me and that I needed to be left alone. She didn't ask me to help wash the dishes after dinner, either, but let me go to my room to have some time with Scratchy.

Of course, it was impossible for me to have privacy anywhere in my house. My room was also my brothers' room. No sooner had I settled down on my bed with Scratchy in my arms than they made their appearance.

I tensed, waiting for them to come out with one of their typical wise-guy remarks. But to my surprise, they came over and sat quietly on the edge of my bed.

"Do you think we could—I mean would it be all right with you if we held Scratchy, too?" Joey surprised me by asking.

I looked from him to Ira. Their eyes were sad and solemn.

"You want to hold Scratchy?" I asked, puzzled. "I thought you hated her. I thought you were glad Mom is getting rid of her."

They both shook their heads. "No," said Ira. "We just acted that way when you were around."

"When you weren't home, we would play with her lots of times," said Joey. "We would feed her Cheese Doodles so she would like us. We would hold her and pet her like you do."

"We never hated Scratchy," said Ira. "We only acted that way because we were jealous she was your cat and not ours."

For a moment I stared at my brothers. Was this really Ira and Joey, the terrible twins, talking to me this way? The same twins whose goal always seemed to be to make my life miserable? I couldn't believe it. Maybe it was some sort of trick.

But I had seen how upset my brothers were this afternoon when Scratchy almost got hurt. I had seen them scrape their elbows and knees on the pavement in order to save her. And I saw them now, with tears welling in their eyes as they looked at Scratchy.

Not only that, but Ira had actually admitted they were jealous of me. Imagine, Ira and Joey, the precious twins who got all the attention and all the privileges—Ira and Joey, jealous of me!

I felt all the hard feelings I had built up against my brothers melt away. "Oh. I didn't even know you two wanted a cat," I told them. "Scratchy could have been all of ours all this time!"

"You mean—you mean you would have shared Scratchy with us?" Joey asked in disbelief.

I nodded. Because, at that moment, I actually felt so close to my brothers I would have shared anything with them. "Why not?" I tried to smile, although I was afraid I was going to start to cry in front of them. "Kids have more than one parent, don't they? Scratchy can have more than one owner. She winds up getting extra love that way. That has to be good."

"Does that mean we can be Scratchy's part-owners from now on?" Ira asked hopefully.

"Sure, from now on," I said. I was rewarded by seeing both my brothers' faces light up with a smile. We all smiled at one another until Joey brought up the painful truth.

"But that doesn't give us very much time to be Scratchy's owners. Tomorrow is supposed to be her last day."

"I know." I leaned back against my pillows and sighed. I rubbed Scratchy between her ears while Ira and Joey patted her back. "If only we could come up with a plan to save our cat!"

It was then that Mom poked her head in through the doorway. "Oh, there you are, Linda. This came in the mail today." She held a printed paper out to me. "I thought you'd like to see it. It's a list of the other campers that will be going to Camp Winnepeg with you, along with their addresses and phone numbers. Maybe there's someone here you already know."

"I already know Brenda Roman," I grumbled. "If she's representative of the kids that are going to be there, I want no part of camp." But I took the list anyhow. I knew Mom was only trying, in her own way, to make me feel better.

She proved it by the next thing she said. "By the way, Linda, your father and I were talking. We decided that you're right when you complain that you have no place in this house you can call your own. You are getting too old to share a room with your brothers. We thought that maybe while you're away at camp we would set up an area in the living room for you. We could put your high-riser in it, a small dresser, and get you a clock radio. We know it's not as good as having your own room, but until we can get a larger apartment, it's the next best thing. What do you say?" She looked at me hopefully.

What did I say? Probably, if it was any other time I would have been overjoyed at my mother's offer to give me my own space. But tonight, nothing could make up for the fact that I was losing Scratchy. Besides, I was feeling so close to my brothers right then that I was almost grateful for having to share a room with them. Once Scratchy left, I would be so alone.

"Fine, Ma. It sounds like a good idea," I said without much enthusiasm. She looked disappointed as she turned and walked out of the room.

I gazed at the list she had given me without interest. What chances were there that anyone I cared about would be going to Camp Winnepeg, anyhow? But sure enough, right there near the top of the list was a name I recognized. And when I saw that name, a wonderful idea came to mind.

"Matthew Bainbridge!" I gasped out loud. "Of course! He's perfect! Why didn't I think of him before?" I was so excited by my discovery that I jumped up off the bed and laughed.

My brothers looked at me as if I were crazy.

"Who's Matthew Bainbridge?" asked Ira.

"And what's he perfect for anyway?" asked Joey.

"Matthew is the boy I ran into at the Fourth of July picnic," I told them. "Remember, he had this huge dog, Winston, who made friends with Scratchy?"

"Uh-huh." My brothers nodded, still puzzled.

"Well, Matthew told me he moved to New Jersey. He has a house with a yard. His family loves pets. When he saw how much fun Winston had with Scratchy, Matthew decided he wanted a cat to keep Winston company."

"And Scratchy would be the perfect cat for Winston." Joey caught on fast. "They already get along!"

"And I remember Matthew saying Scratchy was the best cat he'd ever seen," said Ira. "He's got to want her!"

My brothers and I looked at one another and grinned. We all ran into the kitchen to tell Mom and Dad our idea to save our cat.

Mom was finishing washing the dishes. She looked as sad as I had been feeling just moments before. When we told her our idea, she gave a relieved sigh.

"Why, children, that sounds like a wonderful idea. In fact, I'll call Mrs. Bainbridge and speak to her about Scratchy myself. I'll tell her that if Scratchy has a yard to stay in, she shouldn't be any problem at all!"

I couldn't believe it, but it was only an hour later that Matthew and his parents showed up to get Scratchy. Matthew was really excited about the prospect of taking her home.

"I can't believe it. This is like the answer to my prayers," he told me. "I was so unhappy about leaving Winston at home when I went to camp.

Mom and Dad don't really pay him enough attention, and he'd be by himself in the yard all day. Now, with Scratchy there to keep him company, I won't have to worry about his being lonely."

"And I won't have to worry about Scratchy. I know you'll take good care of her. Won't you?"

"Of course," he said with a grin. "And to make sure I do, you come visit her any time you want to."

"Great." I grinned back at him.

"And what about us?" Ira piped in. "Can we visit her, too?"

"Yeah. Don't forget, we're part owners of Scratchy. For tonight, at least," said Joey.

"I'm not forgetting." I went over and tousled both their heads of hair at the same time.

If I had the choice, of course, I'd still trade my brothers for a cat any old day. But since nobody was giving me the choice, I guess it was better to get along with them.

Besides, I didn't have to worry about my brothers the whole time I was away at camp.

I looked over at Matthew, who was still smiling at me. Now that I knew he was going to be there, the idea of three weeks away at Camp Winnepeg was something I was starting to look forward to!

About the Author

LINDA LEWIS graduated from City College of New York and received her master's degree in special education. *Want to Trade Two Brothers for a Cat?* is her sixth novel about Linda Berman. The other titles are *2 Young 2 Go 4 Boys, We Hate Everything But Boys, Is There Life After Boys?, We Love Only Older Boys,* and *My Heart Belongs to That Boy,* available from Archway Paperbacks. Recently she moved from New York to Lauderdale-by-the-Sea, Florida. She is married and has two children.